"Ben was standing there helplessly staring at the stone wall when something struck his arm, forcing it back against the rock, and then the sound of the shot cracked the silence. With the sound still echoing, Ben shuffled back into the protection of the slab and stood plastered against it. Moving his arm only a little, he stared in amazement at a small purplish hole in it halfway between his wrist and elbow."

ROBB WHITE was born in the Philippine Islands, where his father was a missionary. After resigning his commission in the Navy, Mr. White began the adventurous wanderings which have taken him around the world. He has written many short stories and twenty-two books, including *The Survivor, Silent Ship, Silent Sea, Up Periscope,* and *Our Virgin Island.*

ALSO AVAILABLE IN LAUREL-LEAF BOOKS:

Deathwatch

Robb White

Published by
Bantam Doubleday Dell Books for Young Readers
a division of
Bantam Doubleday Dell Publishing Group, Inc.
1540 Broadway
New York, New York 10036

The trademark Laurel-Leaf Library® is registered in the U.S. Patent and Trademark Office.

The trademark Dell® is registered in the U.S. Patent and Trademark Office.

ISBN: 0-440-91740-9

Reprinted by arrangement with Doubleday Books for Young Readers.

Printed in the United States of America

RL: 5.6

November 1973

OPM 61 60 59

This book is for my wife Joan

Deathwatch

1

"THERE HE IS!" Madec whispered. "Keep still!"

There had been a movement up on the ridge of the mountain. For a moment something had appeared between two rock outcrops.

"I didn't see any horns," Ben said.

"Keep quiet!" Madec whispered fiercely.

Ben crouched behind a boulder and watched this man get into position on his stomach, his legs apart, the heavy rifle resting on a small, flat stone. Madec slowly lowered his face to the cheek piece and eased his hand down to the trigger. Now he lay motionless, looking through the long, fattened telescope sight.

Ben had never known bighorn sheep to behave this way. There had been five of them on the ridge but something had alarmed them and they had disappeared. By now they should be half a mile from here and still going.

"I'd wait until I saw some horns," Ben whispered.

Without raising his cheek from the stock, Madec said, "I saw horns."

"I didn't."

"You weren't looking."

"I was looking."

"Not through a ten-power scope."

Ben stayed crouched, hanging his weight on the sling of his little .22 Hornet. The range was at least three hundred yards, but this man Madec was dangerous with a gun. On the way into the desert Madec had shot at anything that moved—and some things, like a Gila monster lying peacefully in the shade, that did not move. And Madec did not miss. The gun was a beautifully made .358 Magnum Mauser action on a Winchester 70 stock with enough power to knock down an elephant—or turn a sleeping Gila monster into a splatter. A bighorn hit with that gun would drop where he stood. Ben hoped that whatever it was up there would not show itself again.

Madec huddled over the gun. There was an intensity in his eyes far beyond that of just hunting a sheep. It was the look of murder.

There weren't many bighorn left in the world and Ben couldn't understand why anyone would want to kill one, and yet, for the past three days, that was all this Madec had thought about. Killing a bighorn and having the head mounted to hang on the wall of his office in Los Angeles.

"Ben, my young friend, you're not the type of man who can understand big-game hunting," Madec had told him the first night in the desert.

Ben had looked at Madec's face in the firelight, the skin seeming cold even in that warm, soft glow. "The only hunting I understand is when it's the only way you can get something to eat," Ben had said. "Since we don't need one for camp meat, shooting a bighorn doesn't sound like a big deal to me."

That had really teed Madec off. "You may not know it, but the chances of getting a permit to kill a bighorn are about one in a million. I've been waiting for years hoping my name would be drawn from among the thousands of guys putting in for one. When you come out into this desert and risk your life stalking one of the smartest and wariest animals in the world, and you outsmart him and take him on his own ground, you've accomplished something. That's something you'll never understand."

Madec had irritated Ben from the start, and he was sorry now that he had agreed to come out here with him, although he needed the money Madec was going to pay him; it meant a semester in college, maybe two.

"We can go back to town tonight," Ben had told him, "and you can get a guide who thinks the way you do."

"A local-yokel hotshot I don't need," Madec had said. "All I want is somebody to show me where the bighorn are, and they said in town you knew as much about their range as anybody."

"If this is a big competition between you and a sheep," Ben had said, "wouldn't you feel a lot better doing it by yourself?"

"Look, my permit only gives me seven days to

kill a bighorn, and I could spend all seven of them roaming around out here and not even find one. You know where they range, and I'm paying you to take me there. From then on it's just me and them, and I don't need some sand-dune expert telling me what to do."

Ben looked at Madec sprawled on the ground. For three days and two nights Ben had been in the desert with this man, and the only time he had ever laughed was after he told some story about how smart he was. Madec never lost a business deal, according to Madec, and in every deal somebody got hurt. It wasn't enough for Madec to outwit somebody, outdeal a man in some tricky way, the guy had to get really hurt, too.

Listening to Madec made Ben glad he wasn't in the same world as this man. In Ben's town on the edge of the desert there wasn't anything for a man like Madec to wheel and deal for. And, Ben thought, even after I'm a geologist and working for some big oil company, I still won't be in the same world as men like Madec.

Ben looked down at his Jeep on the flat desert far below them. The heat around it made it seem as though it were underwater, the shape of it wavery and indistinct.

Four more days of this man. But he was getting paid for every one of them.

Ben relaxed and listened to the silence. The heat seemed to have killed every sound. It was as though he were in an enormous bowl of silence; as though from the purple mountains sixty miles east to the brown mountains forty miles west all sound had been silenced by the intense, still heat. Even a plane from Edwards Air Force Base, the plane itself invisible, moved in silence, leaving two thin white lines across the hot blue sky.

The sound of the gun was absolutely enormous. It was as though it had shattered the ground and cracked the blue vault of the sky and rolled the mountains back. The thing roared and echoed and lunged into the silence and seemed to roll on, mile after mile, never to stop.

And then, just as suddenly, there was the dead silence again.

Madec's voice sounded small and flat after the great roar of the gun. He didn't even seem interested in what he was saying. "Well, I got him." He was still lying prone as he worked the bolt, the brass empty flicking out and sailing end over end, then tinkling down among the stones at Ben's feet. He reached down and picked it up, tossing it from hand to hand, for it was still hot from the explosion and the desert.

Madec rose slowly and pulled the rifle up by the sling. He took the lens caps out of his pocket and carefully fitted them on the ends of the scope. "Your uncle tells me you're working to get money to go to college," Madec said.

"That's right," Ben said, wondering why Madec suddenly wanted to chat.

Madec dropped the clip out of the gun and slowly replaced the cartridge. "You want to make a deal?" he asked.

Ben watched him shove the clip back in and hit it with the flat of his hand.

Madec looked up. "Well?"

"What sort of deal?"

"Money," Madec said. "For school. You see, Ben, this is the only chance I'll ever get for a bighorn. They'll never pull my name out of that hat again, not in a million years. So, naturally, I want a good specimen, a ram with a really good rack I can be proud of."

"You said you saw horns."

"I did, but not for long enough to tell whether a tip had been broken off, or they were all chipped up from fighting. You never can tell until you've really examined them, you know."

"What's the deal?"

"It really doesn't even involve you," Madec told him. "But I'm giving up a week of my time and going to a lot of expense to get a good specimen. That's all I want. So let's go take a look at what I killed. But if it isn't a good specimen . . ." Madec stood looking at him, smiling now.

Ben thought of the bighorn. He usually saw them when the sun was low and the hard blue of the sky was fading into broad bands of soft colors and the mountains were turning purple. They would stand on the ridges then, probably looking a lot bigger than they really were. Just standing there against the sky looking as though they owned the desert, the huge, curved horns beautifully balanced. He had a feeling that when he and Madec got to the top of the ridge that sheep, with a .358 Magnum through it, was going to look small and forlorn, pitiful. A bloody thing lying among the hot stones, the big horns twisting its neck into some awkward position.

"If it's not the specimen you want I don't report anything, and we just go on hunting for four more days. Is that it?" Ben asked.

"It's not up to you to report anything anyway, is it?" Madec asked. "I'm the hunter here. Right?"

"Right," Ben said. "But I don't want any part of you going around shooting every bighorn in the desert until you get the specimen you want."

Madec laughed. "Ben, now you know as well as I do that I probably won't even get another shot at one. So don't be a Boy Scout. If this isn't a good specimen how about—for double the money and a hundred-dollar bonus—we keep on hunting? If we don't find anything we'll come back and pick up this one. And you still get the extra money. Okay?"

Ben remembered Madec's stories about the deals he made. Somebody always got cheated—and hurt.

But there were mountains where the bighorn never went. Mountains that looked exactly like these. Madec could spend the rest of his life looking for bighorn in those ranges and never find one.

"Okay," Ben said.

"After all, I'm not asking you to do anything

illegal, Ben. I'm just paying you some nice money to drive me around. There's nothing wrong with that."

"Not a thing," Ben said.

"Then it's a deal," Madec said, slinging the gun over his shoulder.

Ben watched him start up the ridge, his feet on the stones making a lot of noise in the silence of the place. Ben knew now that whatever was lying there on the ridge wasn't going to be good enough for Madec. It could be the biggest ram in the mountains but it wouldn't be good enough.

Ben looked around, picking out landmarks so he could find this place again. As far as he was concerned, Madec had seen the last bighorn he was going to see, and whatever he had killed up there was going to be all he killed.

Madec was well ahead of him as he started climbing, the heat blasting down on him as though it had real weight.

Ben had reached a little area of shale, the flat rocks sliding under his boots, when Madec got to the top and disappeared behind a boulder, so that only the muzzle of the .358 could be seen moving along.

A patch of pale brown showed lying in a crack of the cliff face, and as Ben looked down at where they had been he had to admit that Madec had done a good job of shooting.

He was not surprised to see Madec coming back, in such a hurry that he almost fell. Ben waited for him, wondering what he was going to say about the sheep he'd killed. That the horns weren't big enough? Or were chipped?

Okay, Ben thought, four more days of you, but you've seen your last bighorn.

"What do you know?" Madec said, not even stopping as he went down the mountain. "I missed him. I thought I had him cold, but I missed him."

Ben looked at the man in disgust. He must have killed a ewe or a young ram with no rack at all and now didn't want to admit it. "You didn't miss him," Ben said. "He's lying right there in the crack in that cliff."

"No," Madec said over his shoulder as he kept on going down. "I thought that was a sheep, too, but it's only a rock. I missed. Must have jarred the scope climbing up here or this heat got to it, because ordinarily I don't miss a shot like that. Let's go see if we can find that herd again." At last Madec stopped and turned around. "You've still got your deal if that's what's worrying you."

"That's not what's worrying me," Ben said.

"So let's go! If we can get around these mountains before sunset we might see 'em again."

Ben looked up at what he had thought was a dead sheep. What difference did it make to him that Madec was a liar?

"I'm not paying you to stand around," Madec snapped. "I'm paying you to hunt bighorn. So move it!"

"The thing that interests me," Ben said quietly,

"is that rocks don't bleed much." He pointed with his thumb at the pale stone of the cliff. From the bottom of the V where the stone had cracked, a trickle of blood, very dark red in the hot sunlight, ran slowly, the heat congealing it on the stone face.

Madec, his head down, walked slowly back up to where Ben was standing. Then he lifted his eyes and grinned. "I'm a liar, Ben. I didn't miss that shot. Remember, you told me to look for horns, and I said I'd seen 'em. I was lying then, too. I shot a little female. I just didn't want to tell you because I was afraid you'd call off the hunt. You understand that, don't you, Ben?"

Ben shrugged. "Okay, I'll bury it."

"Why bother?"

"Because the game warden will spot her from his chopper and know who killed her, is one reason. You want some more?"

"You can't see her from the air. I had a hard time finding her. I was right on top of her before I saw her.

"You're not a game warden," Ben said and kept on climbing.

"Ben," Madec said.

Ben kept moving.

"Ben!"

Ben glanced back at him.

"We'll lose the rest of the day," Madec said. "I'd rather take my chances with the game warden than lose a whole day just burying a dead sheep. Come on, buddy, let's get going."

The trouble with Madec is, Ben thought, he's always right. There really wasn't much point in lugging that dead weight down the mountainside to bury it in the sand. Here the vultures would be at it by dawn. By nightfall the coyotes would be there, and soon there would be nothing left but a few scattered bones which the rodents would in time destroy.

And what difference does it make to me, Ben thought, if the Game and Fish Department gets all over this guy?

He looked up once more at the blood, now dried on the stone.

He was closer to the broken stone of the cliff now and his angle of vision was different, so that he saw farther into the fissure of the stone.

A white-haired man was looking back at him. His eyes were a faded, skim-milk blue and were wide open. His mouth was open, too, and from it a trail of blood went down his cheek and out onto the rock.

2

THE .358 MAGNUM bullet had done fearful damage, blasting the man's lungs out through his back.

He was an old man who had been in the desert a long time, for the skin of his neck was copper colored and tough looking, old, tanned leather. His felt hat, almost completely stained with sweat, had fallen half off so that Ben could see the sparse white, unwashed hair, the pale skin of the head ending in a sharp line where it met the copper. He had on a brownish wool shirt with long sleeves buttoned at his wrists and a pair of denim pants faded to the color of his eyes. One hand still gripped the handle of the metal locator which lay out in front of him, the round pan of it shining.

Ben knelt and turned him gently onto his back, the hat now falling completely off so that the sun shone down hard on the open eyes and grizzled cheeks. The few teeth he had left were long, stained, worn fangs. Suspenders, one loop shot away, held up his pants.

The clothes lay on what was left of the man in loose folds.

Ben had never seen this man before and wondered a little about that because he knew most of the old prospectors who still roamed these lonely hills, not even hoping any more, just roaming, happier in the desert than in the peopled land.

"I know you won't believe me," Madec said, standing behind him and looking down at the man. "But I just glanced once and saw that there were no horns and didn't look any farther. I just assumed I'd shot a ewe."

"You didn't." Ben put the old man's hat over his face.

"Do you know him?"

"No," Ben said, standing up.

He didn't look at Madec as he picked up the Hornet and said, "I'll go down and bring the Jeep up as high as I can. Then I'll bring the groundsheet, and we can tie it to the rifles and get him down."

"Why not leave the rifle," Madec said, reaching for the Hornet. "You don't need it."

Ben handed it to him and went down the short face of the cliff and on down across the shale bed.

He tried not to think of Madec at all as he climbed down the long slope of the mountain, picking out a path for the Jeep as he went. Instead, he made a mental list of what they would need—the groundsheet, some rope, a blanket to wrap the body in. He debated about that, though, wondering for a moment why it was necessary to stain a blanket, but decided it was.

It was going to be past midnight before they got the body down to the Jeep and got out of the desert. Who should he get in touch with first, Ben wondered. The sheriff? The Highway Patrol? The justice of the peace? Maybe Madec knew.

Poor old man, all by himself out there. All alone with the empty desert stretching out for miles. Walking along, crouched over a little, holding the locator out and close to the ground, listening hour after hour for the buzz that gold or silver would make but never hearing it and never, really, expecting to hear it. Just out there to be by himself.

The Jeep was hot and hard to start, but he got it going and headed back toward the slope of the mountain. He could see no sign of Madec, only the white cliff face with the V now casting a dark shadow.

It was a funny thing about these old prospectors. They only had one life—the desert. They never told you where they had come from before they came to the desert. They never told you of their childhood or their children or wives or parents. If they had ever played a game or gone to school or loved someone, you didn't find it out from them. The only life they had was the last trip they had made into the desert, and the one they were now getting ready to make.

And every one of them had found his gold mine —once. Gold so pure it was lying shining on the ground. They had marked it well, claim-staked it, and then pinpointed it with landmarks of mountains or Bishop pines that had been growing in place for a thousand years. Marked and located their gold so well they could come back and find it in the dark.

Except that when they did come back with a new grubstake and equipment they never could find that place again; no gold lay where they had seen it, only rocks and sand.

One-name old men. Sam, Hardrock, Walt, Zeke. No last name, no known address other than Death Valley or Mohave or Sonora. Any desert. No next of kin.

It took Ben half an hour to wrestle the Jeep up the slope, getting it up as high as he could, not wanting to carry the weight of the man any farther than he had to in the afternoon heat. But when the slope became so steep that there was danger of the Jeep rolling over, he turned it around, heading it down the hill again, and then got the gear and started walking.

He was halfway there with still no sign of Madec when he heard the shot.

Instinctively Ben ducked behind a boulder and then felt embarrassed. There was no telling what Madec was shooting at now, but it wasn't at him.

The rifle cracked again, and Ben only listened to it as he kept on climbing. It wasn't the roar of the .358, it was the Hornet with that sharp, snapping sound.

Idiot, Ben thought, one shoulder sweating under the folds of the nylon groundsheet, the other under the coil of rope and the wool blanket.

Madec was sitting on the ground in what shade there was. He had the Hornet across his knees, looking at it as Ben climbed up to the flat and walked over to him.

"What are you shooting at now?"

"Nice little machine," Madec said, holding up the Hornet. "I'd never shot one before. Good flat trajectory. What's the muzzle velocity?"

He had moved the dead man so that he was half-sitting against a boulder, his ruined body slumped back against the rock, his head hanging down on his chest.

"Enough," Ben said, dumping the groundsheet and unfolding it. "We'll make a stretcher."

Madec didn't move. "You wouldn't believe in this day and age that a man could go around with no identification at all. No driver's license, no social security card." He laughed. "Not even any credit cards. There isn't a thing to identify him. And he hasn't got a dime."

Ben folded the two edges of the sheet over so that they met in the middle and then began to lace them together with the rope.

"No name," Madec said. "No number. Nobody."

Ben glanced over at him sitting in the shade, the Hornet across his knees, the .358 lying beside his leg. It was going to be awkward carrying the old man with nothing to hold the rifles apart.

"All these old geezers wandering around out here are running away from something," Madec said. "Their wives, the law, the people they owe money to. Nobody knows who they really are. And a man as old as this has been out here so long nobody cares."

Ben left the rope long enough at both ends to tie the body between the rifles and then went over to the old man and spread the blanket out on the ground beside him. "Give me a hand, Madec. We'll roll him in the blanket and then lash him between the rifles."

Madec didn't move. "Let's talk a little, Ben."

"What about?"

"This thing was a pure accident, you know that, Ben."

"I don't know what it was," Ben said. "Some people don't shoot at something just because it moves."

"Oh, come on," Madec said. "I thought it was a bighorn. You thought it was a bighorn. We'd just seen 'em standing right here. I thought when they moved that we'd scared 'em. How was I to know that this old man was what had really scared 'em?"

"Okay," Ben said. "It was an accident. So let's get him down the mountain."

"That's what I want to talk about, Ben. This old man with no name, no nothing, is dead. There's nothing we can do about that."

The old man had no socks, and one boot was laced with a piece of wire. Ben lifted him, the desert flies swarming up into his face, and laid him down on the blanket. When he pulled his arm out from under the body it was smeared with dirt and blood.

"Not a thing," Madec said. "And it really doesn't matter, does it? I know that sounds pretty cold-blooded; but it's a fact, Ben. Nobody cared whether this old man lived or died. Nobody is waiting for him to come home because his only home was out here in the desert."

Ben angrily drove the flies off with a corner of the blanket and then wrapped it around him, covering the staring eyes, the open mouth, the mess. The flies settled down on the blanket.

"Are you going to help me with this?" he asked.

"Let's think this thing through, Ben," Madec said. "If we take this old man back to town, it's going to start a big hassle. A hassle that doesn't need to get started and doesn't mean anything in the end anyway. It's just that the law has to go through all these motions regardless. They've got to have their trial with the judge and the lawyers and the total waste of time and money. And after they've obeyed all the little rules, what happens? The death is accidental; it's nobody's fault, not mine, not yours. . . ."

"It sure isn't mine," Ben said.

"Of course not. So after they spend weeks going through all the motions, where are we? Right back where we started with an old man nobody wanted when he was alive and nobody wants now that he's dead. Nobody gets punished, there's nobody I can pay to make their sorrow less, because nobody cares. I ask you, Ben, why put ourselves through all that hassle?"

"You mean you just want to leave him lying here?" Ben asked.

"No! No! We'll give him a decent burial. I'm a religious man and I'll pray for him."

Ben looked down at him. "I hope I never meet anyone else like you."

"That's not a kind thing to say, Ben. Believe me, if I thought this old man had any sort of family I'd find them, and I'd see to it that they never wanted for anything money could buy. Think for a minute, Ben. You've been in this desert all your life, but you've never seen this old man before. Right? You don't know who he is, and I don't think anybody does. Just an old derelict. So let's don't get ourselves all involved in a big legal tangle. You want to go back to school pretty soon, don't you? Well, if you get tied up in this thing you'll be lucky to get back to school *next* year."

"How did I get into this all of a sudden?" Ben asked. "I didn't shoot anybody."

Madec smiled at him. "I can see that you've never been involved with the police. As a witness to this thing you're involved now and, believe me, they can drag it out for weeks, for months!"

"Are you going to help me with this?" Ben asked.

Madec sat there, his back against the rock, and looked at Ben. Finally, his voice low and sad, he said, "I see. You want me to be punished, don't you? Well, I can understand that, Ben. Even though it was an accident, you think I should be punished for it."

"I don't care whether you get punished or not," Ben said. "I haven't even thought about it. All I know is that when somebody gets shot you tell the sheriff. That's the way it is."

"That's the way they *say* it is. I'm trying to get you to see the point of this thing, Ben. The law isn't going to punish anybody. All the law is going to do is find out whether this was a murder or an accident. Now you know as well as I do that it wasn't murder. So why *bother?* I'm going to be perfectly frank with you, Ben. I simply cannot afford to get tied up in a legal hassle. It's worth a lot to me not to waste all that time. So if it's worth a lot to me, I'll see to it that it's worth a lot to you. How much do you need to go to school until you get your degree?"

"Not much."

"You name it, it's yours."

"Give me the rifles."

Madec picked up the .358 and got to his feet. He slung the Hornet over his shoulder. "Ben, I'm going to ask you one more time. . . ."

"You don't need to," Ben said. "The way I see it, somebody got shot, so we're going to the sheriff about it."

"I said, Ben, that I was going to ask you one more time to see this thing my way. If you do, I'll make it so you get all the college you need to get your degree and, after you've got it, I'll see to it that you get a job with the oil company you choose. Now that's a good deal, Ben, so don't turn it down for some petty law."

"I don't want any deals with you," Ben told him. "And I don't care if you're a little inconvenienced because you shot a man. I'm going to the sheriff."

Madec cradled the .358 in his arm and reached into his pocket. "This is the .358 slug that killed him," he said, holding out his hand.

The heavy bullet was just a blob of lead and brass.

"So?" Ben asked.

"Unwrap him," Madec said, putting the slug back in his pocket.

"Why?"

"I want to show you something."

Ben unfolded the blanket.

"He was hit in the chest," Madec said.

"I know that."

"He was hit in the throat, too."

Ben saw the small, blackish wound in the leathery skin of the man's throat.

He couldn't believe this; he couldn't begin to think about it.

"There's a .358 slug in my pocket," Madec said. "And there are two Hornet slugs around here someplace. And two Hornet empties down the hill a way."

Ben folded the blanket back over the old man and stood up.

Madec now had the .358 in both hands, the muzzle down, the fingers of his right hand lying relaxed on the trigger guard.

"Whoever shot that old man," Madec said quietly, "didn't do it accidentally, Ben. You don't shoot a man accidentally twice."

3

"BEN, MY YOUNG FRIEND," Madec said, resting against the boulder, the rifle still poised in his hands, "we haven't been thinking this little event all the way through."

"You have," Ben said. "What are you trying to do, make it look like the Hornet killed this man?"

"You see," Madec said patiently, "you're doing the same thing I've been doing—jumping to conclusions without examining the facts. So now I suggest that we both just cool off and start right from the beginning. Go through it, step by step, and see what we come up with."

"Why don't we start from right here?" Ben asked. "You pick up his feet, and I'll pick up his head and we get him out of here. Because nobody is going to believe that a .22 Hornet blew a man's lungs out of his back."

Madec's voice had a chiding, teacherlike quality. "You are not list-en-ing, Ben. You're not thinking things through. For example, it could be that, long after this man had been shot and killed, he was shot again, with a .358, to, perhaps, create a little confusion. Or to put the blame on someone else. And, don't forget, coyotes and vultures can do a lot of damage, destroy a lot of evidence."

"Not if they don't get to him."

"You've got a point there," Madec agreed. "But let's see if I haven't got one, too. You see, Ben, it just occurred to me that people in a small, isolated community may think differently from people accustomed to the big-city way of doing things." He suddenly laughed. "There's another thing, too, which you may have noticed. There's something about me—I don't know what it is—that sometimes irritates people."

"I know what it is," Ben said quietly. "You give people the idea that if you don't already own it, you can buy it."

"That's probably it," Madec said. "I guess I do throw my weight around a little. And that's what I'm worried about, Ben. You see, if we take this old man in to town there's going to be a trial. And it could just possibly be that the people involved might be a little prejudiced. Even a little envious because I'm better off than they are. A jury chosen from people in a little isolated desert town are naturally going to be biased against a man like me. Don't you think so, Ben?"

"I think so."

"So, there's that. And—there's this. The trial with a prejudiced jury and perhaps even a biased judge is going to hinge on whether or not the death of this old man was *completely* an accident. Now you and I know that there was no intent to kill this man. But, in a trial, the question is going to come up whether or not the death could have been avoided. Now, if a jury decides from the evidence that, although I had no intention of killing this man, the accident *could* have been avoided, then that puts a different light on things. You follow?"

"Madec, you've got a lot better chance just being honest about this than trying to make people in my town believe that this man was killed by two shots from a Hornet," Ben said.

"Ben, I'm surprised. I thought you'd have noticed by now that I don't take chances. For example, using your rifle is what you could call a contingency, something that may or may not come in handy later. It's nothing for you to be concerned about now. What I'm talking about is what might happen if we go along with your plan and take the body back to town. I'm talking about the trial they'll have, the jury. Now that jury could twist things around a little, Ben. They could take what you say at the trial and make it mean more than you wanted. In fact," Madec said, smiling at him, "you're a little prejudiced yourself, Ben, and that might show. Your testimony about what happened would be absolutely honest, I know that. But your prejudice might just tinge it enough to make the jury think that, perhaps, this accident could have been avoided."

Madec shifted his position against the boulder and looked over at Ben. "We did have a little conversation about seeing horns. Now if you repeated that to a group of men who have spent their lives in the desert they might decide that it wasn't just a casual remark you made, but that you had advised me not to shoot. Even that you had *warned* me not to shoot. Now, if your testimony made them think that that was the way it was, then they would logically decide that this was not completely an accident."

"You're not thinking very straight, either," Ben told him. "Just because it's a little town way out in the desert doesn't make the people meaner or dumber than anywhere else. They'll believe the truth when they hear it just as fast as anybody else. And if you think they envy you being a dude from the city you're wrong about that, too. They like it where they live, that's why they live there."

"I wish I could believe that," Madec said. "But, as I told you, I don't take chances. Your testimony at that trial could get me put in jail, Ben."

"What do you want? For me to forget you told me you'd seen horns?"

"I am offended," Madec said. "I resent your thinking I'd ask you to perjure yourself in a court of law. But I'm glad you agree with me that your testimony could result in my being convicted. Convicted and sent to prison, Ben. I have no intention of going to prison. It is not convenient."

"I wonder if this old man thought it was convenient for him to get shot?"

Madec glanced down at the rolled blanket and

then shifted the .358 a little, bringing the muzzle higher. "I don't think I'm getting through to you, Ben. So, tell me this, is it true that people stranded in the desert sometimes get hysterical and take their clothes off?"

What Ben felt was not exactly fear, or even apprehension. It was more physical; a chill gripping his shoulder blades. He realized now that he had known ever since he'd seen the black wound of the Hornet bullet that this was going to happen.

It made him feel helpless and stupid, for the time had passed when he should have made decisions, taken action, protected himself. Now it was too late.

"I've heard that," he said.

"Then you'd better give me your hat, Ben."

Now it was fear. Acknowledging it, recognizing it, turned all the vague apprehensions into sharp, clean fear.

He had been stupid to let Madec get this far without facing this thing, *thinking* about it.

"That isn't going to work," Ben said.

"It will work. Give me your hat and your shirt, Ben. Your boots, too."

"If I don't?"

"Then you force me to make a decision which" —Madec began to smile—"of course, I've already made. Believe me, Ben, I don't like doing this. It's just something that has to be done. *How* it's going to be done I'm going to leave entirely up to you."

Madec's thumb moved slowly and deliberately. Ben watched the blued steel safety catch flip up.

Madec's forefinger went into the trigger guard and moved down to lie on the curved trigger.

It was still difficult for Ben to realize that a man could plan a thing like this; could be so coldly deliberate about it.

"Perhaps it will help you in your decision," Madec said, "for you to know exactly what I plan to do."

"I think I know," Ben said. "You're going to make this look like murder. You've already done that"—he nodded toward the blanket—"with him. Now you're going to make sure I can't deny it."

"Good thinking," Madec said. "Very precise. So let me tell you what my thinking on this is. Or do you care to know?"

Ben thought about the Jeep and was disgusted with himself. But how could he have known that this insane thing was going to happen?

On each side of the Jeep for at least a hundred yards and downhill for more than that there was nothing but open ground. No place to hide and the shale would trip him if he tried to run. The .358 would stop him before he got halfway to the Jeep.

"I'd like to know," Ben said.

"It's simply this. You're an honest, law-abiding young man. Therefore I can't trust you. We could make a deal here to forget the conversation about the horns. But, in court, under oath, your honesty would be put to a severe test. I can't risk that."

"What you're doing is a lot riskier."

"No. You see, the fact must be established that you, not I, shot this old man. The way we do it I leave entirely up to you so let's discuss the alternatives. First, I could shoot you now. That might seem the simplest and quickest solution, but the trouble with a thing like that is it takes planning. There are a lot of details that have to be fitted very precisely. There's always the chance in a premeditated murder to make a fatal mistake. So, unless you insist on it, let's eliminate murder, shall we?"

"Good idea," Ben said.

"The second way is for you to take off your boots, your shirt and your hat and put them on the ground. Then empty your pockets. You can keep your trousers on, but not your socks. How far is it to the nearest highway?"

Ben looked to the west. The mountains were black now with the sun setting behind them. "About forty-five miles."

"Good. So, with no clothes to protect you from the sun, and no shoes to protect your feet, and with no food and no water, you've got a long walk."

"I'll make it," Ben said.

"Perhaps. It really doesn't matter. Because, if you do, the story you tell and the story I tell are going to be quite different."

"Madec," Ben said quietly, "do you really

think that the people in my hometown are going to believe you when you tell them I deliberately shot an old prospector I'd never seen before in my life?"

"Perhaps they won't," Madec said. "But here's the beauty of it, Ben. They certainly are not going to believe your story. Nobody will believe that a man could treat another man the way I'm going to treat you. They'll have to doubt your story because, when you think about it a little, you'll see how insane and illogical it will be. On the other hand, my own story will be so logical and sensible it'll be hard not to believe it.

"All of which," Madec went on, "isn't really important because I don't think you can survive those forty-five miles, Ben. With no water? I'll see to it that you don't get any. As a matter of fact, I'll harass you all the way."

Ben couldn't believe any of this. And in the still, heavy heat and absolute silence he began to wonder if Madec had said any of it.

"You're nuts, Madec," he said. "Come on, let's get this old man in the Jeep."

It was as though the small rock his right foot was on had suddenly been hit by a sledgehammer. The blow numbed his foot halfway up his leg and from there on sent sharp tingles of pain all the way into his stomach.

Ben looked down at the hole in the ground where the rock had been and, as though remembering it, heard the explosion of the .358.

He lowered his numb foot, watching to see when it was back on the ground and then looked over at Madec.

"What's your decision, Ben?" Madec asked quietly, shoving the bolt home on a fresh cartridge.

Ben stood without moving, studying him. Suddenly the feeling of helplessness, the confusion, even the fear were gone. Oddly, he felt nothing about Madec—no hatred, not even dislike. The man had ceased to exist except as part of this problem he now had to handle.

Ben realized that he had no choice at all. To make any sort of move toward the gun or toward escape would only get him killed.

He flipped his hat over at Madec's feet and then peeled off his shirt. Standing first on one leg and then the other, he took off his boots and socks and dropped them on the ground. Then he emptied his pockets, turning each one out as he did so. When he was stripped to the waist, barefoot and bareheaded, he looked at Madec. "Okay?"

Madec said, pleasantly, "I've changed my mind, Ben."

"Now you're making sense," Ben said.

"Take off your trousers, too. You can keep your shorts on. And off with the sunglasses."

Ben started to unbuckle his belt and then stopped. "Can you kill a person just to keep from answering a few questions? Just to keep from maybe going to jail for a few months?"

"Who are you?" Madec asked, his voice still pleasant. "Are you real smart in school? Are you a genius, or something?"

It felt strange to Ben to be thinking at this time of the B's and a few A's he had made. "I'm not a genius."

"You're just a young kid. Twenty-two. I asked about you before I hired you. Nice kid, hard working, wants to be a geologist. No parents. No wife. Lots of girls but no real girl friend. During the last three days out here with you I've found out a lot more about you. You're a nobody, Ben. And you'll never be anything but a nobody. You're a loser, Ben. The world is already too full of men like you."

"There's one too many of you, too," Ben said.

"Some people agree with you," Madec said quietly. "But who am I? I'm president and sole owner of a corporation in California. Not a huge thing like General Motors, but I employ about six hundred people. I'm married, and I've got two wonderful children. Now all of these people, my six hundred employees, my wife, my children, depend on me for the food they eat, for their shelter—for their lives. I'm important to all those people and, in my business, it would be absolutely ruinous for me to be put in jail on any charge at all for any time at all, even a day. You see, I'm looking out not only for myself but for all those other people. I'm balancing them against you, and you lose."

He held out his hand and Ben dropped his

trousers and stepped out of them and then
dropped his sunglasses down on them.

"All right," Madec said. "Go. But remember
this, Ben. I'll be watching you every step of the
way. You're not going to make it."

Ben looked at him once more and then walked
away across the flat top of the ridge. The smooth
stone was hot under his feet, and he could feel
the heat of the dying sun on his bare skin.

As he walked, the muscles of his back cringed,
waiting for the first touch of that heavy .358
slug. He could feel his flesh puckering in antici-
pation.

The slope down from the ridge was not as
steep on this side as the one they had climbed,
and he walked slowly, picking his way through
loose, sharp rocks.

There was not a sound anywhere.

The open area ended in a jumble of boulders,
and he moved in among them, hurrying a little
now, for he wanted the feel of thick stone between his back and the gun.

Beyond the boulders was a narrow arroyo, and
he dropped down into it and went along it until
he was sure he was out of sight of the ridge.

Then he turned around and, crouching, went
back upward, moving carefully and slowly
among the water-washed stones as he followed the
trench of the arroyo back toward Madec.

When the arroyo became too shallow for good
concealment he stopped and very slowly raised
his head until he could see through a narrow

crack where two boulders lay together.

Madec was not there.

It was a small satisfaction, but as Ben studied the ridge he thought, Okay, Madec, now you've made your first mistake.

He could not see the old man from where he was but, as he settled down to wait, he remembered the boots. Good boots and about his size.

4

THIS WAS A TRAP. Standing on the highest point of the little range of mountains, really only hills rising perhaps a thousand feet from the desert floor, Ben studied the trap.

The sun was now well behind the western range, those distant and, he knew, difficult mountains, black as coal against the dying sky. Beyond that range, forty-five miles by crow flight from where he stood, there was a highway and, fifteen miles farther on, a town.

A trap, an enormous bowl, the bottom of it open, rough desert, the sides mountains. Like a little pile of lettuce in the center of a salad bowl were the stubby little mountains where he stood. A Jeep could circle entirely around them in half an hour, and a man with binoculars could see anything that moved on them.

Between Ben and the high range to the west there were thirty-five miles of open desert. Not a perfectly flat land of hard-packed, almost concrete-smooth sand, like the dry lakes around Edwards Air Force Base, but open enough for a man in a Jeep to see a man on foot trying to make his way across all those miles.

Ben kept turning slowly, the blood on his cut feet dried hard and flaking off. Around the entire compass there was no route that did not include miles of open desert.

Ben could not yet accept this situation. He still could not believe that anyone would deliberately kill a man just to avoid a trial which, at worst, would put him in jail for a few months. And he could not rid himself of the hope that Madec would change his mind. That, with time, he would realize that this crime he was committing could be far more dangerous than the accidental shooting of the old man.

To make the hope real he realized now that he must give Madec time to think, time to reconsider. With the shooting so recent and this plan of Madec's so new it would be dangerous to provoke him now.

The trouble was that Ben had very little time to give away. He could not afford to let Madec rest and contemplate, provided with plenty of food and water and protection from the sun.

With no water Ben's body could stand this heat for only two days; probably less than that since he had no clothing to protect him and contain his sweat.

If he could find a catch basin somewhere in these hills and could squeeze as much as a quart of water out of the sand, it would do him no good at all. A quart of water would not add even an hour to the forty-eight hours he could hope to live.

Even if he were lucky and found two quarts—a half gallon of water—it would not really help, adding only an hour or so to his life.

To survive here for as long as two and a half days would require that he find a full gallon of water. To make it for three days he would have to have more than two gallons of water. Four days—five gallons.

And he didn't even have two full days. He had already used up eight of his forty-eight hours, for he had not had a drink of water since before they started stalking the bighorn.

As he turned to go down the slope, Ben saw the headlight beams of the Jeep stab out like a pale knifeblade across the stony floor of the desert.

Ben stood where he was and watched the Jeep scurrying along the base of the mountains, then turning behind the western end of the range.

He must think I've started across the desert, Ben decided.

That's your second mistake, Madec.

Ben moved down the ridge, picking his way carefully, his feet now swollen and painful. He knew that he should give this problem more than just the hope that time would change Madec's mind. He should be attacking it from every angle. Instead he could think only of small and unimportant things. He needed shoes and clothes. He needed water. He was hungry.

It took him a long time in the dark to get back

to the ridge where the old man had been shot.
Ben decided that he could use the groundsheet,
the rope and the blanket but not those bloody,
smeared clothes. Just the boots. He could cut a
poncho out of the blanket.

Madec had moved the body back to where it
had first fallen.

The groundsheet, the rope, and the blanket
were gone. The man's old felt hat was gone. So
were all his clothes.

In the starlight the old man's bare feet looked
naked and white, with a dark line of dirty skin
at the ankles.

The voice in the darkness sounded very close,
but as Ben listened, he realized that Madec was
thirty or forty feet away, concealed behind a jumble of boulders.

"I'll put his shoes and hat and clothes back
on," Madec said, "after you don't need them any
more."

"Madec!" Ben cried. "This isn't the way to do
it! People are going to ask too many questions."

Ben heard the shale clicking as Madec went
down the slope. Going to the cliff, Ben watched
him heading straight down to the Jeep.

Ben knew it was useless, but he searched the
ground all around the dead man, searched the
whole area of the ridge, hoping that Madec had
made the mistake of just hiding the stuff somewhere.

He had not made that mistake.

Ben went to the edge of the cliff again and

looked down. Madec had the Coleman lantern lit, and Ben could see him moving around, cooking his supper over a campfire. He had told Ben the first night that that was more "fitting" than using the Primus stove.

Moving until he could no longer see the old man, Ben sat down with his back against a slab of stone and waited.

The moon seemed to hang behind the black mountains, shy and undecided, allowing only a weak glow to show that it was there at all. But, at last, it came plunging up, enormous, faintly tinged with a reddish-brown color, only a small part of its roundness still dark in the earth's shadow.

The moonlight was not bright enough for him to make out the old man's tracks or even those of the bighorn, but Ben hoped that his own years in the desert would help him now.

An old prospector like that would make a good camp. It would be in the lee of a cliff and would have a view of the desert. It wouldn't be close enough to any water hole to scare the game away but close enough to bag a quail or a rabbit when he needed one.

Ben got up and started picking his way carefully, the moonlight helping him keep his feet off the sharp rocks. At the same time he searched for any mark; the scrape of a boot nail on a stone, the darker earth where a foot had overturned a rock, any trace of digging where, perhaps, the metal locator had buzzed.

What had the old man found? A beer can left by some hunter? A brass empty where someone had fired a shot? Gold? Silver? Nothing?

Once, when Ben was a boy, an old prospector people called Hardrock showed up at his uncle's filling station. Hardrock had once been a burro man but had given up the little burros and for a while had gone on foot. But, that night, he showed up with what they called a "mule," an overgrown motor scooter with a big rear wheel and tire, an air-cooled engine and a beefed-up frame.

Broke, Hardrock had borrowed five gallons of gas from Ben's uncle, who had also loaned him five dollars. As collateral Hardrock insisted on leaving a good, sheepskin-lined coat.

That coat had hung in the closet in Ben's uncle's house for ten years, and then Hardrock, now in a pickup truck, had appeared again. He paid for the five gallons of gas, returned the five-dollar loan, and took back his coat.

Almost at the end of the range and halfway down it Ben found the old man's camp. He had not expected to find much. A groundsheet and blanket or, if he was a real dude, a sleeping bag. The cast-iron Dutch oven a prospector couldn't get along without. A shovel to fry meat on. Dried apples, beef jerky, flour, salt and pepper. Depending on how long he'd been out, some cans of tomatoes, chile beans, perhaps a slab of bacon. He'd have a rifle, usually an old .30-.30, and a pan to wash gold with, a couple of changes of clothes and, always, a water bag or jerry can and a jug of vinegar to clear the water with.

Madec had found the camp first.

Ben felt a childish rage. This wasn't fair! Madec was breaking the rules.

Madec had left very little. No sleeping bag, no blanket, no groundsheet. No clothes of any sort, no shoes. No food. He had smashed the Dutch oven with a rock. If the old man had had any tools or a gun Madec had taken them.

Ben felt like a man coming home to find his house burned to the ground.

He was turning away, not knowing where to go, or what to do when he spotted the five-gallon water can. The old man had set it in a crevice to keep the sun off it.

Just the sight of the can gave Ben an almost savage pleasure. He yanked it out of the crevice and unscrewed the cap.

It was empty.

For a moment he was too stunned and disappointed and angry to think, but as he automatically untangled the little chain attached to the cap and screwed the cap back on he realized that, at last, Madec *had* made a mistake. With this can, if Ben found water, he could save what he couldn't drink.

It pleased him. The look and feel of the can was good. It had a nice, smooth, rugged handle set flush in the top and was easy to carry.

If I can find enough water to fill this can, he thought with rising excitement, I can forget Madec and just head for home. If I can get water he's not smart enough to stop me.

Feeling satisfaction at the heft of the can he swung it up.

Madec had smashed the bottom out of it, breaking the welded seam so that the piece of metal that had formed the bottom was bent up inside the can.

Ben put it down very gently, as though not to hurt the bottom any more. Then he sat down on it, his feet bleeding again, staining the moonlight on the stones.

Gradually, just sitting there, he began to feel smaller, helpless, a naked child threatened not only by the desert but by a grown man intent on killing him.

There was no way to outwit this man Madec.

What can I do? Ben thought. I can walk on down this hill and across the desert and over to the Jeep where the Coleman lantern is burning and food is cooking and there are gallons of fresh water. I can tell Madec that at the trial I will say anything he wants me to say, leave out anything he wants me to leave out. That we had no conversation about not shooting before he saw the horns. That I, too, was sure his target was one of the bighorn we had just seen there. I can promise him on my honor that I will convince any jury that the death of the old man was an accident, complete and total and unavoidable.

It wouldn't work. Madec was not the kind of

man who could trust another man to keep his word.

Ben leaned back and stared up at the stars. Even they seemed to have withdrawn from him. On the ridge the stars had seemed so close, so friendly. But now, with the moonlight suffusing the black sky, the stars had moved millions and millions of miles away from him. And were not concerned with this threat to his life.

Not wanting to look any more at the hostile stars, he lowered his head and in so doing saw something alien, something that did not belong where it was.

For a moment his eyes couldn't find the place again, but as he searched where he had been looking he saw it.

Perhaps, Ben thought as he got to his feet, the old man had used this same water can to stand on, for the ledge in the cliff was at least eight feet above the ground and Ben, who was six feet tall, could not reach beyond the base of the ledge and had to take the can to stand on.

On the ledge there was an ordinary little tin box with a bright metal handle. His uncle kept one much like it in the office of the filling station to stow the credit card slips in.

It was locked, and Ben couldn't force it open with his bare hands.

As he looked around for a rock to break it open, his pleasure at finding the box began to fade. Madec had searched that old man, looking for some identification. He must have found the key to this box in the old man's pocket or on a string around his neck. Wherever he had it Madec had found it.

Ben set the box on edge and began hammering it with the rock.

There's going to be nothing inside this box. There's no use going to all this effort to break it open. Madec would have looked for what that key fitted. He would have found this box and now it would be empty.

Or perhaps Madec had left him a little token inside, something to let Ben know that he had been outwitted again.

The lock at last broke apart and he pried the bent lid open.

Something alive sprang out of the box and Ben threw the thing away from him, leaping back from it as the box clanked against the stone cliff and rattled down to the ground, the thing inside writhing in coils around it.

Ben moved farther away from it, unable to see in the shadow, but guessing that it was some sort of snake Madec had found, a sidewinder or a small diamondback.

Without taking his eyes off the ground between him and the box, he stooped and picked up a stone. Holding it ready, he studied the ground, watching for any movement.

The snake didn't come out of the shadow so Ben went carefully back toward it, very conscious of his bare feet and ankles.

Nothing moved and there was no sound of rattling or hissing but now he could see the coils of the snake, part of it apparently still in the box.

Ben watched it for a long time, wondering why it did not move again.

At last, not taking his eyes off the snake, he stooped and felt around on the ground until he found some small pebbles.

Straightening, he selected one and tossed it over at the snake. It struck the box with a little tinkling sound.

The snake did not move.

Ben threw the handful of pebbles at it.

Nothing moved.

Going back to where the old man's campfire had been, he found a charred piece of mesquite about two feet long. Using that as a sort of rake, he drew the box out of the shadow into the full moonlight.

The snake was rubber. Rubber tubing, Ben found when he picked it up. It was attached to a metal framework of some sort which, until he held it up in the moonlight, he couldn't identify.

The thing was a slingshot but like none he had ever seen before. This one not only had the grip you held in your hand, but also a metal extension with a curved flat piece of aluminum on the end. When he finally figured it out, he found that the extension formed an arm brace.

A formidable machine, the rubber not in bands

but stout, round tubes. Drawing the leather cup back, he was surprised by the strength of the thing.

A good shot could probably kill something as big as a jackrabbit, and that was what the old man had probably used it for.

It had a nice, solid feel, and he stood, flexing the rubber tubes, the frame solidly braced in his hand and along his arm.

It's a weapon, he realized suddenly. Not a gun, not even a bow and arrow, but at least a weapon.

A small, round stone thrown by this thing and hitting a man in the head could do some damage.

Putting the slingshot aside he went back to the box.

There was a little transistor radio in it but he had broken it smashing open the box. There were some spare batteries for the locator and a leather tobacco pouch. In that were a couple of dozen double-O buckshot; big, round lead pellets. Ammo for the slingshot.

In the bottom of the box was a plastic billfold. Ben took it out and went through it. In a pocket with a snap on it was 85 cents in coins; in the money slot there were two one-dollar bills and one twenty-dollar bill, very limp and old.

In another compartment there was a snapshot of a young man and woman sitting on the steps of a porch. The man was wearing a suit and tie. Lower on the steps were two little children, a boy and a girl. There was nothing written on the picture.

There was nothing else in the box.

Ben replaced everything except the slingshot and tobacco pouch and put the box beside the water can where it would be found if anyone ever came here again.

Picking up the slingshot, he fitted it back into his hand and along his arm and tested its power again.

I'll have to practice, he decided. When I get time I'll have to learn to use this thing.

But first I'll have to find water. If I don't do that soon I won't need to practice shooting a slingshot. I won't have time enough.

5

BEN HAD GIVEN UP hope of finding water. He stood on the edge of the cliff and thought bitterly that even the bighorn were against him. The big sheep had left a well-worn trail along the ridge of the mountains which he had been able to follow even in the predawn light, and such a trail should have led to water. Instead, it came to this cliff and ended, sign of bighorn going off in all directions.

It was a trick, Ben thought. Like Madec, they were playing with him; killing him.

Without water there was no contest. All Madec had to do was wait out the few remaining hours.

For the first time Ben felt a deep, almost paralyzing fear. It was not the sharp, mouth-drying fear he'd felt walking away from Madec and expecting the bullet to slam into him. This fear was deep inside him, a huge, dark fear; a foreboding.

And then when the first light of the sun touched the ground at the base of the cliff he saw the catch basin. A small one, a hollowed area in the rock perhaps ten feet across and, he guessed,

not more than three or four feet deep. Bighorn
tracks were all around it. To get to the water,
they had pawed the sand out of the hollow so that
it formed a sort of fan around the basin.

As he looked down, the dark fear inside him
seemed to shrink a little, to withdraw a little. Not
fifty feet from him there was water. Not much,
the hollow was small and shallow and the bighorn had been working it, but the sand showed
some dampness.

And he had better implements than the bighorn; his hands were more efficient than their
hooves and could do a better job. With his hands
he could scoop the sand out of the natural bowl
which slow erosion had formed in the rock. He
would have to squeeze the dampness out of each
handful of sand until, when all the sand was
scooped out, there would be a little bitter-tasting
muddy water collected there from the rains of a
month or so ago.

To reach the basin he had a choice of getting
down the cliff, which was about twelve feet high,
or walking along it until it merged again into the
mass of the mountain, descending in an easier
slope. Ordinarily this would have been a simple
decision. Now he stood for a long time, measur-
ing distances with his eyes and gauging the pain
in his body.

Looking over the edge of the vertical cliff, he
could see a rubble of sharp, broken stones at the
foot of it with fresh sand scattered on them by
the bighorn. To hang by his hands and drop the

last four or five feet onto those stones was going to hurt and probably add new cuts to his already lacerated feet.

On the other hand it was a long and painful walk along the cliff and down and then back to the basin. A time-consuming walk and, with the sun already above the eastern mountains, he didn't have much time before the real heat hit him.

From the top of the cliff he could see the Jeep parked at the base of the mountains. Madec had made a neat camp there, putting up the tent and stretching the canvas awning. There was no sign of him, but he could easily be sitting comfortably in the canvas folding chair in the deep shade under the awning, watching him.

Ben got down on his hands and knees and eased his body over the edge of the cliff, slowing the swing downward with his legs and knees rather than with his sore feet.

Even when he was hanging by his hands from the cliff edge, he hesitated, the idea of the impact of his feet on the stones below holding him plastered against the cliff face.

Whatever it was smacked into the cliff with a hard, dry sound. A little cloud of dust, the rock particles big enough to see, leaped out from the flat stone face, hung a second, and then dropped away.

Ben knew that he had been hit even as he let go and dropped. It seemed to him as he fell that he had been hit even before he heard the sound and saw the dust, although he knew that it had not been that way.

Something had hit him high on the cheek, hard enough to push his head to one side but not with the force of a bullet.

Falling, he realized that it had been either a chip of rock from the face of the cliff, broken off by the bullet, or a part of the bullet itself, shattered and ricocheting.

Then, still falling, he heard the sound of the rifle.

Madec was shooting at him with the Hornet, not the .358. In a box in the Jeep he had a hundred rounds for the Hornet. Madec had started with twenty-five rounds for the big gun and had about a dozen left.

At the first contact with the ground, Ben made his legs and knees go limp so that he landed almost collapsed, his hands taking some of the weight.

The pain made him grunt out loud.

Blood running down his chest suddenly made him aware of the pain in his cheek. He felt it lightly with his fingertips but could only tell that there was an open cut about an inch long just below his eye.

There were new cuts on his feet also; one of them near his ankle was bleeding rather badly.

Even squatting there he had a view of the camp below, and now saw that Madec was kneeling in the back of the Jeep, the Hornet lying across the canvas top.

Ben felt a wave of defeat as he pushed himself up with his hands and at last stood straight. He could not tell from here whether the catch basin was in view of the Hornet's scope, but as he started toward it he had a strange feeling of inevitability. The basin would be in easy range and clear view. Ben just knew that.

This time he heard the bullet go past him. It was so close that he heard not only the sharp little *click* noise it made in flight but the actual sound on the stone beyond him.

Then the crack of the rifle rolled lazily up to him.

Would Madec deliberately shoot him, he wondered.

Ben decided that he had to find out.

Ignoring the pain in his feet, he leapt forward, running as hard as he could toward the catch basin.

Little noisy explosions on the cliff face went ahead of him all the way, the bullets missing him by inches.

The man was a good shot, leading his target very accurately.

Ben threw himself forward on his stomach. The catch basin was at the bottom of a small depression and when he lay flat down this way perhaps Madec could not see him.

There was silence from the desert as Ben inched forward, using his bare elbows against the stones.

The bullet struck just in front of his face, filling his eyes with sharp, dry dust which smelled of ozone.

Ben pushed on, reaching out to the edge of the basin.

The bullet knocked rocks out from under his fingers.

Madec was now standing on the hood of the Jeep, his arm in the rifle sling.

That was not as good as having the rifle barrel resting across the top of the Jeep. Not as steady. A little gust of wind, a little tremor from a heartbeat and, whether Madec wanted it to or not, the bullet would hit him.

A piece of quartz just in front of his eyes suddenly split open, showering him with bright crystals.

Even if he was not hit directly by a bullet these sharp slivers of rock flying around could take his eyes out.

Ben rolled over on his back and sat up, waving his arms around. Then he pushed himself up to his feet.

Ben made a helpless gesture with his arms and turned away from the basin, walking slowly, picking his way.

As he went back to the top of the range he studied the bighorn sign, hoping to find another trail that would lead him to another water hole but, except for the trail he had followed there was only sign of aimless wanderings.

Near the summit he sat down in the shade on the western side of an outcrop of stone.

He found with his fingers that his face had stopped bleeding. The flesh around the cut was painful now, and he could tell that it was swelling.

His feet were in bad shape, old cuts broken open, new cuts still bleeding.

The slow, small irritating desert flies arrived and swirled around him. They were so stupid, so suicidal, but killing them only seemed to make them increase in number. They wandered in and out of his wounds or sat and preened their wings or even bred, flitting in his blood, and there was very little he could do. They had made a home on him.

The Jeep was moving. To Ben it seemed as though the cloud of light brown dust was pushing the white body of the Jeep forward, bouncing it along on the desert.

About a mile from the mountains where he was, an old eroded butte rose at an angle from a low cut terrace. Ben watched Madec force the Jeep up the sloping wall of the terrace and, once on it, turn the Jeep so that it was facing him. Madec got out and although Ben could not see exactly what he was doing, it appeared that he was slowly scanning the area ahead of him.

Ben had studied that butte and cut terrace in the moonlight, realizing that its location made it a serious threat to anything he might want to do. He had hoped that Madec, without the panorama he had, would not recognize the advantage the terrace would give him.

It depressed Ben to see the Jeep parked there; Madec now back under the shelter of the roof, invisible in the heavy shadow.

From the terrace Madec could see the entire south side of Ben's little mountain range, from the eastern to the western end. He could also see the wide stretch of open desert between Ben's small range and the high ranges in the distance which surrounded this egg-shaped bowl of desert.

From Madec's vantage point the only area he could not see was to the north of the mountain range.

A man with sufficient water and food, with clothing to protect him from the sun, with good boots on uninjured feet and sunglasses to keep his eyes from burning out, could escape from Madec by simply going down the north side of the mountains and hiking out across the desert, heading due north so as to keep the mountains between him and Madec.

An injured man, almost naked, with no water and no food, could not venture into that northern area. For at least a hundred miles there was nothing but open desert, worn and gently rolling, the surface of the ground littered with small rocks and stones with, here and there, the sprouts of the tenacious and enduring desert plants.

There would be no catch basins of water out there. There were not even any barrel cactus, the water-soaked flesh of which could keep a man alive—provided he could somehow cut through the leather-tough skin of the plant.

To the north was the only route he could take and not be seen by Madec, but as things stood now with almost twenty-four of his forty-eight hours of life already gone, he could not survive ten of those hundred long miles.

Ben realized that Madec must have come to the same conclusion, and so he sat watching through the binoculars, knowing that Ben had only three choices:

To stay where he was, some water near him but made unavailable to him by the Hornet.

To come down from the mountains and start walking across the desert to the east. (Madec would not even have to move the Jeep but could just sit up there on the cut terrace and watch Ben die somewhere out in those empty sixty-five miles.)

Or to come down and walk to the west. (Naked and with no water there was small difference between sixty-five miles one way and thirty-five the other.)

Almost numb to the aggravation of these flies walking around on his face, Ben looked across through the heat-shimmering air at the white Jeep. It seemed poised and ready to go—to follow him, grinding along slowly in four-wheel drive.

Ben tried to remember how much water Madec had but gave up, realizing that he had far more than enough to outlast him.

And there was gas enough to keep the Jeep roaming around for at least a hundred miles in four-wheel, two hundred in two-wheel.

Mechanics, machines, supplies were not a part of this game. In the final analysis, even the guns were not a part of it.

Sitting in the hot, still heat, the flies crawling endlessly on him, Ben felt everything dropping away.

He thought of search parties he had been on looking for tourists who had left the main highways to do a little rock-hounding or have a picnic. People who had allowed some small accident like a stalled car or a broken axle to kill them.

He remembered a little family of four, parents and two children, who had died on the desert within sight of the highway.

That family had done everything wrong. When their car stalled and they couldn't get it started again they had walked away from it, leaving five or six gallons of dirty but drinkable water in the radiator. They had walked away from the shade it could have given them, walked away from the evidence of trouble the search party would look for. And they had walked away in the daylight, in the sunlight, in the killing heat.

When Ben found them it had almost made him cry to see how the mother had smeared lipstick on the faces of her children in a futile effort to keep the sun from burning the flesh off them. . . .

Ben had always thought that he could survive in this desert he knew so well as long as he could move.

He could move, if you called stumbling on

those torn feet moving. He could move for about twenty-four hours more, and that was all.

All night long he had hoped that with the coming of day Madec would realize that he was making a fatal mistake. That to kill Ben out here would be far more dangerous than confessing the accident and taking his chances with a jury.

Now Ben admitted to himself that Madec, as intelligent as he was, was too vain to give up. Vain and conceited and sure of himself, sure that he could convince the authorities that Ben had killed a man.

Madec would tell a simple, convincing story. Ben had killed the man and when Madec had insisted on reporting it to the authorities had tried to kill him, too. But Madec had escaped to the Jeep and made his way back.

Madec would tell it well, Ben decided. All the details would fit; he might even go so far as to wound himself to make it more convincing.

Madec would see to it that all the evidence supported him. The old man, ruined by vultures by the time they found him, would be wearing his clothes again and his boots and hat. The two Hornet slugs would be easy to find.

Ben would also have his clothes on. Madec would find him where he had at last dropped and would dress him and equip him—with empty canteens and gun and food.

It was too late now for any reconciliation, too late to just walk off this mountain and go to Madec and beg for his life.

He fought back the fear. As long as there's water on this mountain, he told himself, I'm not dead.

Tonight, he planned, when the moon goes down, I'll go back to that catch basin. To keep Madec from seeing me I'll crawl all the way there on my stomach.

But I'll get there.

With the dry heat pressing in on him from every direction, Ben relaxed against the outcrop and forced himself to stop the squirrel cage thinking; to empty his mind and sleep.

6

AT FIRST Ben didn't know what had waked him, but he awoke with dread, as though some enemy was close on him, threatening him.

His wounded cheek had swollen so badly that his left eye was completely closed and he could not, even with his fingers, open it enough to see out of it.

It was still daylight, the sun seeming to be squatting on the western mountains, no longer moving down but staying there, pouring its heat on him.

Then he heard the sound and realized that was what had waked him up. A tinkling sound. Of metal on rock.

Pushing himself up a little, his head toward the sound and turned far enough to see with his right eye, he looked down.

Ben could only see Madec's head and shoulders and could not tell what he was doing.

Pushing himself on up, pain throbbing into his legs, he looked around the outcrop.

He could see Madec clearly now. The big

Magnum was propped not far from him against the cliff face, and Madec, his fancy bush jacket dark with sweat, was using the Jeep's short-handled shovel.

It was insulting, infuriating. And Ben felt a strange, weak, childish thing. Don't *do* that, he silently begged. Don't do that.

Madec had shoveled most of the sand out of the catch basin and was sloshing out the rest, the sand-filled water looking dull and gray in the sunlight as it flew from the shovel and splashed down on the bare, sloping, hot stone. The water ran down the stone in a little shallow stream, vanishing as it ran.

Madec shoveled and scooped until the basin was empty, the sand all around it drying fast in the dying sunlight, turning from an almost black dampness to the faint brown of the dry sand.

Holding to the rock with his hands to keep the weight off his feet, Ben moved back behind the outcrop and slowly let himself down again.

Now all his hope for miracles was gone and Ben was left with a strange and chilling thought.

He and this man Madec were locked together, chained together in a struggle for life itself—a struggle with no niceties, no rules of behavior, no sportsmanship, no gentlemanly conduct.

Madec could not leave him. The struggle had gone too far for that. Nor, on the other hand, could Ben escape. Without water he could not make it across the miles of open desert, and, even if he had water, his feet could not endure that distance. In ten miles the flesh of his feet would be worn away down to the bones.

The Jeep was the key to life. The man with the Jeep would live, the other man would die. There were water, protection, food, movement, communications, weapons and comfort with the Jeep. With the Jeep one man could kill the other.

Madec had the Jeep.

Ben sat watching Madec walking back to the Jeep, the gun over one shoulder, the shovel swinging in his hand. He looked so satisfied with himself, so jaunty in that cocked-up Australian hat.

Ben had been close to death a few times. On highways, on a high crag, once in a helicopter when the rotor clipped a treetop. The closeness could be measured in inches or seconds, and death had gone past him before he actually recognized how close it had been. At those times, the fear came after death had gone and he could, in safety, think back to what might have happened.

Now it was different. Death was close and he knew that, but now he had time; he could sit here and think about it; could feel it coming, slowly, minute by minute, hour by hour.

In his mouth and throat he could feel death as a strange, unwettable dryness which his saliva could not diminish. He could feel it in the swelling of his tongue which had started back in his throat and seemed about to choke him with its dry mass.

Twenty more hours?

Or was it only nineteen now?

The sun had finally started moving down behind those huge mountains to the west. Like a hand stretched out to help him a long, thin and almost rectangular shadow came steadily across the desert toward him. Ben followed the movement of the shadow with his eyes.

Three hundred million years ago the place where he now sat had been submerged beneath an inland sea, and the plateau at the foot of the mountains had been a great marsh covered with weird and enormous mosses and ferns. Then the first animals with backbones had appeared—strange fish—and later there were reptiles in the swamps.

At this time the great eruptions, the immense flowings of lava, the extrusion of mountains from the almost fluid surface of the earth had quieted, and the climate became cold. All the northern world lay under thousands of feet of solid ice.

Two hundred million years ago dinosaurs had walked where the Jeep now sat and six million years later tyrannosaurus, lizards that stood twenty feet high and had fearsome claws and teeth, roamed what was then almost all marshland, lying under a cool and rainy climate.

And then, about sixty million years ago, the earth here had become violent again. The whole chain of the Rocky Mountains was vomited upward and volcanoes erupted and built themselves up and died and were eroded away by wind and water. At this time the climate was mild and pleasant and the first horses had appeared, hardly as big as basset hounds, with toes rather than hooves.

At some point during all the violence of prehistory there had been a volcano about seven miles from where Ben sat. Rock, melted by the intense heat of the earth's deep interior, had been pushed upward by unimaginable pressures and had broken through the cool crust of the earth at that place.

This molten rock, called magma, had been forced upward with great violence, filling the sky with a fountain of stone so hot it flowed like water. And, like water, the stone had fallen back around the hole in the earth, slowly forming a cone of cooling rock, building up layer by layer into the conical shape of a volcano.

Even as this mountain of once-molten rock was forming, magma continued to be pushed upward, not only through the hole in the earth but on up through the hole in the conical mountain.

Gradually then, as the pressure beneath the earth diminished, a solid core of rock filled the hole in the mountain. This rock, because it cooled more slowly than the lava exposed on all sides to the outside climate, formed a harder, more dense stone, basalt.

As the volcano died, the winds, loaded with fine particles of sand and pumice from the volcanoes, began to erode its conical sides, and rain ran down the slopes, washing them slowly away, and cold, which froze the water caught in stone cracks, split and splintered the surface, and a sea rose and lapped at the top of the basalt core.

Until, at last, there was nothing left of the high, conical, lava mountain except this core, the plug of the volcano. It towered straight up from the floor of the desert, steep-sided, erect, slender. A monument to those ancient times of violence. A tombstone.

And its shadow beckoned him, its shape haunted his mind.

Ben estimated the butte to be about four hundred feet tall and half a mile in circumference. In some places enormous, almost flat-surfaced slabs had been broken away and lay scattered on the desert below, making a rubble of stone called breccia around the base. The breaking away of these thin slabs had left flat ledges like giant steps up the sides of the butte, and other erosive elements, such as the cold of the glacial period, had split the surface stone, leaving long, perpendicular cracks in the sides.

The top of the butte had been worn flat.

There was little on that monument of stone to interest an animal, no vegetation for the bighorn and so no carcasses for the coyotes; no reason for a cougar to lurk there. Vultures might use it for a roost, snakes would investigate the cracks for lizards and rats. But that stony pinnacle would be home for few.

In the morning the butte had been a beautiful reddish copper color, the areas where the slabs had broken away looking almost golden. Now, with the sun behind it, the face toward him was a deep, dark purple.

With his one seeing eye Ben studied the butte and the desert floor around it. He studied the landmarks of rain-cut arroyos, mountain peaks, the small mesas, other buttes.

The one whose shadow reached out to him was the most majestic of them and, with the sun setting behind it, almost seemed to move toward him as the stone merged with the shadow.

Now the sun was completely behind the butte, turning it into a tower of blackness.

And then a single brilliant ray of light appeared to come straight through the solid stone of the butte. It lasted for only a moment and then the stone was solid and black again.

That was all Ben needed to see and for a second he felt a great triumph, for he knew now where he was going.

He turned his head and looked down at Madec.

The whole desert was tinged with a soft red glow. Even the white Jeep was pink now and Madec, moving around his camp, was a tiny, red-tinged man.

Darkness came very slowly as Ben sat there, waiting. But at last the sunset faded and the moonless sky grew black and the stars began to appear.

Ben picked up the slingshot and pouch and pulled himself up. Then he set out, going down the northern flank of the mountains so that Madec could not see him.

He had not gone far before doubt began to eat at him. The pain of the stones against his feet was enormous, breathtaking, and he could never tell when some sharp edge was going to send it shooting through him.

But when he at last saw the dark shape of the giant saguaro lying there on the sand, other younger ones standing like dumb, motionless sentinels around it, the going seemed a little easier, the pain a little less.

Oh, little Gila woodpecker, Ben begged, be here. Like this place; make your nests here. I need you.

He had often wondered angrily how a woodpecker could be so much smarter than a man. The Gila woodpecker knew better than to kill a giant saguaro. The bird, like men, left its mark on the great cactus but, unlike men, it never killed one.

A saguaro ten years old is no bigger than a baseball. At twenty-one it is as tall as a man. After seventy-five years of life in the rugged desert it will have grown to twelve feet but it will still be a dwarf among its elders for, after two hundred years, when the saguaro is full grown, it towers fifty feet above the desert, a great thorny stalk of growth, with strong, upright, praying arms.

A man carving his initials in the skin of a

saguaro, initials that will probably never be seen
again by another man, can cause this giant, two-
hundred-year-old plant literally to bleed to death.

And many men have done just that.

The Gila woodpecker, on the other hand,
knows when it is not safe to nest in a saguaro. It
will never injure the plant during the rainy sea-
son for the little bird depends on the saguaro and
will not hurt it.

However, when a nest will do no damage, the
woodpecker cuts a small, round hole through the
tough hide of the plant and works its way into
the saguaro's pulpy, wet interior. Then the bird
hollows out a place for a nest, and the plant
soon coats the walls of the nest with a tough, dry,
corky plaster which not only keeps the moisture
of the plant from running out and thus killing
it, but keeps the nest dry and snug for baby Gila
woodpeckers.

In an old plant there will be dozens of these
nests which, when the plant eventually dies, re-
main, looking like dry, somewhat shapeless
boots.

The moon was coming up when Ben reached
the old cactus, now long dead as it lay on its side
on the floor of the desert. Nothing was left of it
now except a cylindrical cage of what, in the
first moonlight, looked like long, slim fishing
poles. These hollow ribs had once been the pipes
for water storage, pumping water almost as fast
as it was gathered from the roots which often

spread out for sixty feet around the base of the plants.

Now they were bone dry and crackled as he pulled them aside and lifted out one of the woodpecker nests, a tough-skinned, gourd-shaped thing with a hole at one end of it.

Ben worked two of them out from among the dried ribs and, first shaking them carefully to get rid of any scorpions that might be in them, he sat down on the sand and put them on his feet. It was a painful process but once his feet were inside the nests the pain eased and, when he stood up, he knew that, with just that much protection from the stones, he could go ahead.

They would not last long, the corky stuff being brittle and thin, but by walking carefully, picking his way and putting his feet flat down and lifting them straight up, he could move.

There were five more nests and he got them all, carrying them in his arms as he turned west and began to walk.

One by one the nests wore out as he went on westward, the moonlight full on the desert now, making distance deceiving.

Ben passed up the occasional yucca, hoping to see the tall, swablike flower of a sotol rising seven or eight feet above the compact plant.

He had almost given up hope of finding one and, now barefooted again, the last nest worn through, was heading for a yucca when he saw the swab over to his right, the flower stalk standing straight and motionless, shaped like an oversized bottle brush.

Neither the sotol nor the yucca are cacti but are of the lily family. However, the sotol doesn't have the vicious thorn at the end of its leaves that have given the yucca the name Spanish bayonet and the leaves are tougher.

It was a good, young plant and Ben went to work with it. Tearing off a few of the older leaves, he sat down with them and stripped them of their outer edges which were barbed the entire length of the leaf so that they made a sort of double-edged bandsaw blade.

The sharp edges gone, he continued to work with the leaf, pulling off half-inch-wide strips and laying them in a pile. When he had enough he took new leaves and tore them into wider bands. These he wove together, layer on layer, each layer laced to the others with the thinner strips. When the foot-shaped pad was an inch thick, he wove the thin laces across it and then continued adding layers of the woven leaf.

At last he had two clumsy sandals, thick-soled and with laces of leaf strips which he tied around his feet and ankles.

They were painful to walk in but not nearly as painful as being barefoot among the stones.

Gathering more of the leaves, he strung them together and started out again, carrying the bundle of leaves by a knotted strip.

He went on westward toward the butte, the moon now setting, the night far advanced.

Added to the pain of his feet was the increasing pain of thirst. His tongue was very dry and felt as though it had cracked open in places. It filled his entire mouth, a great, stiff swollen mass that pressed against his lips. His throat felt hot and as though coated with dust, and the pain in it came in slow, long-lasting throbs, each one seeming more intense than the one before.

In the fading moonlight the butte seemed as distant as the far mountains, and there was no shadow from it on the desert now. It was still far away, standing silent and somehow, sullen, in the empty desert. It looked ominous and black, threatening, forbidding.

He had to stop occasionally to replace the thongs which kept breaking, and at each stop he could see that the layer of woven leaves between his feet and the stones was thinner.

He had hoped to have covered more ground in the cool of night but, as he walked on, he knew that he would be lucky to reach the area of breccia by dawn.

At this slow pace he might even still be walking in the desert, perfectly visible to Madec from his vantage point on the cut terrace.

There was nothing to gain by turning back and climbing again into the low mountains. He would die there as surely as he would die in the breccia.

There was nothing to do but go on. But not at this slow pace.

It took all his willpower and all his strength to force himself to start running.

He ran awkwardly, the thick, ungainly sandals flopping, the bundle of leaves flapping against him, the slingshot swinging in the moonlight.

From the Jeep, if Madec was watching, Ben would have been a pitiful thing to see; a naked man running in the moonlight across a savage waste of desert.

7

BEN STOOD at the base of the butte and hated it. The black column of stone went straight up into the starlit sky, rising from the rock-strewn desert as though it did not want to be associated with such a place.

The stone of the butte was warm and smooth to his touch. It felt as implacable as the steel door of a vault. There seemed to be no flaw, no crack, no hand- or foothold in the vertical wall. High above him it looked as though the climbing would be easy, but standing here at the base he could find no way to begin, no way to get his body up the first few feet of the smooth, black, silent stone.

He had been all the way around the butte, hoping to find a way up the far side, out of sight of the Jeep, but the far side was even smoother than this side, and there was not a shadow of a crack lower than fifty feet.

Here, in plain view of the Jeep which he could just make out on the terrace, there was a ledge or the edge of a stratum, or a crack—he could not tell what it was with only starlight—about twelve or thirteen feet above him, but he could not reach it. He had felt all along the face of the rock for some crevice or grip but there was none.

Ordinarily it would have only taken some hard work to reach that ledge, but Ben recognized now that he was approaching the last stages of thirst; he was weak with it and spells of dizziness were coming faster. The flesh of his tongue was peeling off and, of all the pains of his body, he was most aware of the aching of his lips.

The first symptoms of severe thirst had come during the time he was running. He had felt then the sudden loss of strength, a lassitude that made him think that he could not possibly raise his foot and swing it forward and put it down again. Even running, and knowing that his life depended on his running, he had felt a desire to sleep—to sleep as he ran, to sleep anywhere, anyhow.

As he began the job of reaching that little ledge, what would have been a simple task was now an enormous obstacle, for he not only had to exert the physical effort, he also had to fight off both sleep and panic.

Ben knew what the next symptoms would be. Toward the end after the lassitude and sleepiness and odd lack of hunger, a man dying of thirst begins to get dizzy. He vomits and his head aches. He aches all over. Finally the intolerable itching begins, an itching which affects every inch of his skin and does not stop until he dies. During this time a man is tortured with hallucinations; he sees water within reach and *knows* that it is there and he will, as many men have, scoop up dry sand with his hands and try to drink it.

Ben hoped he could endure the physical symptoms, but he was afraid of the hallucinations; afraid that he would not recognize them when they came, afraid that there was no way he could stop them or continue to operate rationally through the periods of imagining.

He was a pitiful sight as he worked, naked, at the base of that towering stone monument. Picking up boulders so small that ordinarily he could have thrown them like rocks now required all his strength. Staggering, he lifted and carried each stone to the base of the butte and placed it on the little pile he was building there.

When he thought the pile was high enough he rested for a moment, preparing himself. Afraid that if he sat down he wouldn't be able to get up again, he stood against the butte, his body sagging against it as he tied the slingshot and the sotol leaves together and then strung the tie thong around his neck so that the stuff hung down his back.

Climbing onto his pile of stones he reached up, his hands flat against the smooth rock, his fingers reaching beyond his sight, for his face, too, was flat against the cliff.

His fingers felt nothing, no place that curved inward. Just smooth, warm stone.

Twisting a little so that he could bend his knees, he flattened against the butte again and, taking a deep, sobbing breath, rammed himself upward, his hands groping high above his head, his body scraping upward against the hard rock.

The fingers of his left hand, as though maneuvering separately, found the ledge and snapped over it, reaching in at right angles to the face, until his four fingers were on the ledge and his thumb was pressed flat against the face. His right hand, the fingers scrabbling on the stone, could not make it, and as his upward thrust ended and his body began to drop down again, all he could do was flatten his right hand against the stone. His weight slammed upward through his left arm and concentrated in the four fingers on the ledge.

They held, the dust under them making them slide off to the first knuckle, but then holding.

The sotol sandals defeated him. Trying to pull himself high enough to get a grip with his right hand was impossible, for the sandals gave his feet no purchase at all on the smooth stone.

He could not shake them off but shook them so nearly off that they hung, dangling and now totally useless.

Ben let go and dropped, one sandal twisting his foot savagely when it struck the little pile of rocks.

Rage and defeat and helplessness brought him almost to tears as he tried to untie the knots holding the sandals on. Unable to loosen the knots, he tried breaking the stiff fibers of the sotol leaf but could not do that either and had to return to the knots. It took all his will just to keep his fingers from attacking them wildly and uselessly.

Once the knots were loose he started to throw

the sandals away in a rage but calmed himself and
strung them with the other stuff.

Knowing that he could reach the ledge seemed
to give him strength, and it did not seem as difficult the second time to get a grip there with his
left hand.

Then, the rock tearing at his feet, he swung his
body against the cliff face, everything clinging to
it and moving against it, until his right hand slid
over the edge.

He hung there, his feet bleeding down the rock.
There was a sound close to him and it took a little
while for him to recognize that the odd, whistling
noise was his breath against the stone.

Feeling down from his fingers through all the
muscles of his body, he tried to decide by the
feel, the touch, the thickness of the dust, which of
his hands had the better grip, which the most
strength.

Possibly because his left hand had brushed
away some of the dust when he had let go the first
time, it seemed to him that that hand was the
one to use. The fingers of his left hand seemed
more in contact with the raw stone, more closely
welded to it.

He turned loose slowly with his right hand,
feeling all his weight jam up his left arm, and
grasped his left wrist with the fingers of his right
hand.

Holding tightly, he felt around with his feet
and knees and thighs; he could even feel the muscles of his stomach searching along the stone.

His feet found only small roughnesses, his knees seemed useless.

Pressing his body tight against the stone, he threw himself upward, pulling up hard with his right hand so that the fingers holding the ledge were almost yanked off it.

Blindly his right hand flew over the ledge, his fingers dancing across it, reaching, feeling, searching until his body began to drop, scraping, down again, and he caught the edge with his right hand and stopped falling.

The ledge above him was about a foot wide and slanted a little to the east.

He had so little strength left now that he could not even stop to rest, the pain of his hanging shooting through him, a numbness beginning in the fingers wrapped around the sharp edge.

He began to swing his body like a pendulum from side to side, his stomach and knees and chest scraping as he swung.

He kept swinging in wider and wider arcs until he knew that any more would snatch one hand or the other away from the ledge. At this point he swung as far to the right as he dared and then, instead of letting his body swing downward again, began with all his strength to fight his way on up the side of the stone. With the inside edge of one foot and the outside edge of the other he tried to walk up the face; his knees feeling like blind, fingerless hands grasping at the smooth stone. His skin grabbed the rock and held and pushed, the short beard on his cheek giving it a grip.

His right foot, flying, scrambling up the rock, lost the feel of rock for a second and moved in open space as it passed the ledge. He flung the foot inward, his toes reaching and grabbing, and at the same time, hunching his shoulders, he let go with his right hand and swung his right elbow up over the ledge.

He hung there a moment, his left hand holding, his right elbow and right foot over the edge, his left leg hanging useless below and under his right leg.

That could ruin it, Ben thought, feeling all the separate parts of his body one at a time. With that left leg under his right the only way he could get up on the ledge was to roll himself over. If his left foot had gotten there first it would be easier, he would just have to pull with leg and arm and hand and slide up on the stone step.

It was too late to start over; he did not have that much strength left. If he let his right foot slide off the ledge now, let his body drop down again, he doubted whether he could even keep from falling all the way back down to the desert again. If he did that he knew that he could never get this high again.

The muscles in his arms and legs had started to tremble. It was not the easy shaking, the melted feeling after a sudden burst of exercise, this was a *jerking*, jumping motion, uncontrollable and dangerous, for, with each jerk, his muscles seemed to lose all capacity for tension.

He had to move and could not move. He could

not stay where he was, or go anywhere except down.

For a long time Ben had felt as though he were moving in some sort of thin, pearly fog so that nothing he thought was sharp and clear. Now, for a few seconds, the fog seemed to lift and he could see and feel and think again with an acute sharpness.

He had to go up. Just that simple. *Up.*

If he did not, Madec could sit in the Jeep cracking walnuts on the steering-wheel spokes and watch him die.

Ben tried to move, to roll himself over onto the ledge. He could not do it. He simply did not have strength enough left, and he slumped back, just hanging there by foot and hand and elbows, his body sagging down against the rock.

It was pure, raw rage that at last swept him upward, rolling, sobbing, grabbing with knees and legs and skin and toes.

He was there, lying on his back on the ledge, the edge of it running along his backbone so that half his body lay in space, held there by an arm and a leg down along the face of the butte.

He lay with his eyes closed, his breath coming in hard, dry gasps, his stomach heaving and his muscles painful now with that sharp jerking. Some part of the slingshot was cutting into his back, but he did not have strength enough to move it.

The sun came up as he lay there, the light turning the stone high above him from black to coppery gold. Some birds flew around up there, sometimes lighting on the high stone but mostly flying.

Ben watched the light moving slowly, as though it were some thick, invisible fluid. It came lower and lower, until it touched him, washing over him.

Moving carefully, Ben let first one leg and then the other slip over the edge and hang as he pushed himself up, his back grinding against the stone behind him, until he was upright, the muscles of his butt grasping the stone beneath him.

Looking down, he saw the blood dripping from his feet. It was a beautiful color in the early morning light and looked pretty on the stones below.

His hands were bleeding too and so was his right elbow and the inner surface of both knees, the skin abraded off them as though by a file.

Sitting there, he wished that he could remember exactly when he had last had a drink of water. Had it been just before they left the Jeep to stalk the bighorn? Or had it been before that, say half an hour before? An hour?

It was important to know, and it angered him now that he could not remember.

If it had been just before they left, that would have been close to noon. Assuming that, he still had six more hours.

But had it been earlier?

He grew so angry about this that he began to shake, and he could feel the blood of anger rushing up into his face.

Suddenly Ben stopped it all.

What difference does it make? Six hours. Five. Four.

There was nothing he could do about it and the useless anger he had felt frightened him. Was this the beginning of hallucinations, this anger which had been for a moment a kind of insanity?

It scared him, and he raised his head and looked around.

Madec was standing beside the Jeep relieving himself in the sand.

The sun had cleared the eastern mountains and was already smaller—and hotter.

Looking down, his little pile of rocks seemed remarkably far away, and this pleased him.

The ledge was not more than a foot wide, but the stone slab which had once been a part of it had broken off cleanly so that the top of the ledge was almost perfectly flat.

Twisting his body and pulling with his hands, he got the slingshot and sandals around where he could handle them.

The sandals looked thick and clumsy in the daylight, and he decided that they were too hazardous.

His bare feet were also hazardous, the blood could cause him to slip and, when he was higher on the butte, this could kill him.

He opened the fly of his shorts and tore them along the seam until he could work them out from under him and then down and off his legs. Once off, he tore them in half.

The ledge was so narrow and his perch on it

so insecure that he did not do a very good job of wrapping the pieces of his shorts around his feet and tying them, but when he had finished, he knew that walking would not be as clumsy as with the sandals, although it would be more painful.

Holding his hands flat against the rock, his shoulders pressed against it, he pushed himself up until he was on his feet, spread-eagled as he faced outward.

Madec was now sitting on the hood of the Jeep scanning the range of mountains with the binoculars.

Easing himself along, first one foot and then the other, his back pressing against the stone face, he went upward along the ledge, his hands always in contact with the stone.

For forty or fifty feet it was slow but easy going, the ledge neither widening nor narrowing as his bandaged feet shuffled along in the thin dust, turning it to a damp brown mud which quickly dried.

Looking down, Ben guessed that he had moved up ten or fifteen feet on the ledge incline so that he was now about thirty feet above the breccia.

The ledge ended sharply at a great vertical crack in the butte. Standing at the end of the ledge and craning his neck around the corner, Ben could see only that it was a crack, an open chimney, too wide to jump across and with nothing to land on on the other side.

With his back against the rock he could not look up and so, holding carefully, he turned around so that his chest and knees and stomach were against the butte.

It gave him an odd, shivering feeling to stand this way, his naked back to Madec and his face pressed against the stone. Again he felt his flesh trembling as he waited for the first touch of the bullet.

The only sound was of the birds wheeling around high above him.

The crack was wedge-shaped, wide across on the outside with the two walls coming together on the inside.

The width of the crack where he stood was, Ben estimated, about six feet from wall to wall. The crack was about fifteen feet deep. Above him it seemed to go right to the sky without changing shape, a straight, vertical V of stone, an open-sided chimney, the walls very smooth, almost slippery looking, and since they were not yet in sunlight, impossible to see clearly.

Although he had not noticed it as he moved along the ledge he could now see that it curved a little outward and, as he looked back along it, discovered that it petered out at the lower end, coming finally to a point which blended into the stone face about ten feet above the ground.

Leaning over as far as he could, he looked down the dark chimney.

It shocked him. Although he knew that it could not be more than thirty or forty feet to the bottom, it looked immensely farther than that, a terrifying distance. To fall down it would kill you.

A dark place, the sunlight seeming to have been cut off by a knife as it lay on sharp stones jumbled together and then ended in blackness.

Craning his head back, he looked up along the wall.

There was nothing. For as far up as he could see the stone face was smooth, almost glassy in the sunlight; smooth and golden looking. He did not see a place where he could get so much as a finger grip in that stone.

To be sure he lowered his head, resting it against the wall and reached up with his hands, feeling all over the stone above him.

There was no grip there.

Lowering his arms he looked again at the wide mouth of the V.

It seemed wider now. His guess of six feet across to the other wall seemed short. Seven? Eight?

Turning, his shoulder pressed against the wall, he moved until he was standing sideways, his feet together on the narrow ledge, his side hugging the wall, as he faced the wide opening of the V.

Far away—in another world—he heard the Jeep starter grinding, then grinding again. Finally the motor started, with Madec gunning and choking it. He didn't handle motors well.

Without looking back, Ben inched forward until the front pads of his feet were over the edge of the ledge and only half his arches and his heels still touched the stone.

Then he let himself fall.

Holding his body stiff, his arms out ahead of him, his hands flat open, he fell toward the far wall of the V.

Something was wrong, something was happening that he had not expected. It was all wrong.

And there was nothing he could do about it now.

Then he realized that he had fallen out of the sunlight and was in the darkness of the V.

His hands struck the far wall with much more force than he had expected, and even as his palms and finger pads strained to grip the smooth wall, the weight of his falling body came against them. He felt his hands skidding down and could not stop them.

Ben tried desperately not to let his body sag, to keep his back straight and flat so that he could ram power against his feet, which were still on the cut of the ledge. His hands against the far wall, Ben hung there, slowly sliding down, his body stretched out at full length, the muscles of his stomach gradually loosening and breaking the rigid bridge his body formed as he lay straight across the open end of the V.

He could not hold it, his stomach muscles were jerking again, giving up and letting his body sag downward to add its sliding weight to the thin pressure on his hands.

Below him he could see the exact cutoff line of the sunlight, the stones in it sharp and strongly marked by shadow, the stones directly below him only dim shapes in the shade.

Somehow, never knowing how he did it but knowing he could never do such a thing again, Ben flung himself in toward the angle of the V and as his body moved he turned it, rolling over in the air, his feet scampering along the stone on one side, his outreaching hands scrabbling against it on the other.

He wound up five feet below the ledge, on his back, suspended from his hands and feet which were pressed against the stone, his little bundle of leaves and the slingshot lying on his belly. He arched his back, putting more pressure against the palms of his hands and the soles of his feet.

Moving only one hand or one foot at a time and moving them only an inch or so before slamming the pressure back against them, he edged deeper into the angle of the V, moving until the top of his head scraped the stone and on, his head hard against his chest as his shoulders touched stone, and on until he was compressed into the V, his back against one wall, his knees up against the other.

Ben did not look either up or down as he began working his way higher, the rock face cruel against the skin of his back as he ground his way up.

All of his flesh hurt so that he could not even tell whether the stone grinding the skin off his back was more painful than the skin being ground from his knees and shins and the tops of his feet.

His tongue was now so swollen that it filled his

mouth and overflowed, a huge, purple blob of throbbing, peeling meat outside his mouth, half-clogging his nose. His lips had shreds of flesh hanging from them.

It seemed to him that somebody with a little blowtorch was shooting a tip of flame into the corners of his eyes, and he kept trying not to blink, for there was no moisture to ease the lids across his eyeballs and so they scraped across them, dry and dusty.

What air he could draw in through his half-clogged nose felt like flowing flame going up past his eyes and down his throat, burning away the skin.

He wanted desperately to look up, to see how much farther he had to go, but he forced himself not to raise his head, fearing that the distance left would defeat him.

After a while he seemed to be wrapped in a hard casing of pain. There was no sound any-where except the sound of his choked breathing; there was no light any more; there was no dis-tinct feeling, no reaction of hands and fingers against rock; there was nothing but pain. Time stopped, and distance became meaningless.

He thought of nothing, for it now took no thought to move what had to be moved to advance his body up the stone; it was a slow rhythm, one muscle after another, one bone and then the next, over and over, on and on. Forever.

Ben was not even aware that, for some inches now, his shoulders had been touching nothing, and he almost fell when the pressure of his legs pushed his bare butt out on the level and the change of pressure pitched him forward so that he was hanging, head down, teetering and rocking on the upper end of the V, two hundred feet of emptiness below him.

It was the sunlight that finally made him stop his automatic weak pushings and gropings.

The light burned his eyes when at last he opened them and looked around, his sight blurred and hazy.

Half-rolling, half-sliding along, he moved out of the sun and into the shade, and there he collapsed, lying awkwardly on a flat area of stone, some birds coming down close to look at him.

8

THE SUN WAS the most fearsome thing Ben had ever seen. He could not believe that it could be so high in the absolutely cloudless sky, could not believe that it had taken him so long to get up that chimney of stone.

He looked down at himself, and it made him sick. His feet were just bloody lumps of torn flesh half-covered with the dirty, bloody shreds of cloth.

Where the rock had abraded him, the blood stood like a watery red dew.

And in this juice of his blood the sun, looking small and mean, was frying him.

It was at least eleven o'clock in the morning and, as he pushed himself up, he knew that he could not survive much longer. The itching had started all over his body. He resented most the fact that the itch was the most intolerable where his flesh had already been torn away.

He was very sick and weak and saw now where he had vomited, small shreds of food in a thick, drying slime. He could also see that his hands and

feet were jerking and shaking as though being
moved by something invisible to him.

Forcing his eyes to stay open and to focus instead of rolling helplessly and dizzily in their dry
sockets, Ben saw that he was sitting at one end of
a wide, upward-sloping ledge of stone. Above him
the face of the butte went straight up, apparently
to the top, some hundreds of feet above. The surface of the rock was as smooth as a tombstone.

Looking along the ledge he saw that it ended
abruptly, not fading back into the mass of the
butte, but cut off sharply.

Other than the ledge and the cliff face there
was nothing, no depressions in the stone, no fis-
sures forming shallow baskets. There was nothing
in sight that could interest even the birds.

And there was no shade. There would be shade
late in the afternoon but, by then, it would be
too late to do him any good.

It required a great effort for him to get up on
his feet and when he took a step out along the
ledge, the pain almost drove him back to his
knees.

Doing what he could to support himself with
his hands on the cliff face, Ben hobbled along
the edge until he came to the end of it.

It was like a knife in the back; it was a mean-
ness; he had been cheated, he had been robbed.

The ledge ended as though it had been cut off
by an enormous bandsaw, the edge of it perfectly
straight. And from the edge it dropped straight
down, all the way, right to the breccia; there was

not a break or flaw in the straight wall.

Something, the cold of the glacial ages, or the violence of earthquakes, or the temperature of a certain upflow of magma, had formed in the stone of the butte a shape almost like a funnel standing on end which had been cut in half from top to bottom. The ledge intercepted this stone funnel about halfway up the cup of it. High above him Ben could see the rim of the funnel, very wide there, perhaps a hundred feet across. Below him the spout was a chimney such as the one he had climbed, but instead of being vee-d this one was round, a cylinder cut in half.

From where he stood, it was at least fifty feet across open space to the other side of the bisected funnel, farther than that if you measured across the curved stone face of the funnel itself.

On the other side he could not make out exactly what the formation was, for a thin wall of basalt, a slab which had not broken off stood straight up at the outer edge of the butte, apparently unconnected to the mass except at the base. This thin wall and the solid wall of the butte formed a narrow corridor which lay in deep shade, the slab wall between it and the sun.

It didn't really matter what was in that dark corridor, for he could not get over there.

He could, in fact, go nowhere. He was too close to death now to make it back down that long, vee-d chimney and, even if he had been in his best physical condition, there was no way, without ropes and pitons and hammers, spiked boots and heavy gloves, to climb the sheer face of the butte.

And without someone on the other side to anchor a rope bridge for him, there was no way across that curved bank of stone which formed the cup of the funnel.

Ben was standing there helplessly staring at the stone wall when something struck his arm, forcing it back against the rock, and then the sound of the shot cracked the silence.

With the sound still echoing, Ben shuffled back into the protection of the slab and stood plastered against it.

Moving his arm only a little, he stared in amazement at a small, purplish hole in it halfway between his wrist and his elbow.

Slowly turning his arm over, he saw the other hole, this one more ragged and with a little stream of bright blood flowing out of it and down into the palm of his hand.

There was no pain at all.

Ben put his thumb on one hole, his forefinger on the other and pressed gently. Now there was pain, but nothing compared to the aching of his mouth, or the burning of his eyes, or the sun on his raw flesh.

He moved his arm slowly from the elbow, raising and lowering it and then turning it from side to side. These movements caused no more and no less pain in the wounds.

He drew his hand into a fist, watching his fingers moving easily and normally.

He had been shot. But it did not hurt him, and it had not damaged him. Even the blood had stopped flowing.

Ben had not thought about Madec for a long time. Now he did.

Madec was shooting now to kill him.

And Ben's body falling from this high cliff, smashing down against the ledges and finally into the breccia would be so mangled and broken that no one would suspect that he was dead before he fell.

Faintly, as though from another world, he heard the Jeep engine start.

Madec was trying to find a position where he could see Ben again.

It would not, Ben realized, be hard to do.

Somehow the sound of the Jeep set his mind adrift and he was suddenly thinking of a thing called a Velo-Drome that he had seen at a county fair when he was a boy. A girl with a long red scarf trailing in the wind had ridden a motorcycle up from the bottom of a wooden pit, going around and around until she left the sloping wooden sides and the motorcycle was traveling on the perfectly vertical wall of the thing. He had stared at this, not believing it could be done, but she was doing it, the red scarf trailing straight behind her, as she lay, flat out in space. . . .

In a few minutes, Madec would have maneuvered into position to shoot him again.

Ben knew that he had only until that Jeep motor stopped.

Reaching behind him, he pulled the bundle of sotol leaves and the slingshot around to his stomach. He lashed them all into a compact bundle and then worked the whole thing around to his back again, tying it against his backbone.

Lifting one foot and then the other, he ripped the shreds of his shorts from his feet.

Ready, he stood a second longer, looking out across the ledge at the hot, smooth, slanting face of the funnel.

Far below him the Jeep appeared and braked to a stop, the dust settling around it. Madec got out, moving in the dust.

Ben had an odd, clear thought: I don't want to die here. Not here, on this barren piece of stone.

He came out on the ledge.

He came out fast, pushing himself out with his hands against the wall and, as he ran, he tried to block off the pain which pounded up from his feet.

Whether Madec shot at him or not he would never know, for he seemed to have come into a bright, hot, tiny world, filled with sunshine, stone and silence. He did not hear his own breathing, or the thudding of his feet, or the increasingly hard beat of his heart.

He did not feel anything, not the wind of his movement, or the heat of the sun, or the gentle rubbing of the bundle against his ragged back. All he felt was the soles of his feet, his whole attention moving down to those two areas of flesh and concentrating there.

He ran straight off the end of the ledge, straight out into the sloping stone funnel.

Now the areas of his feet touching hot stone changed. He was no longer running flat-footed; the left outer sole of his left foot and the inner sole of his right were all that touched.

Every sense of feel he had he concentrated there in his feet, feeling every tiny roughness, his skin seeming to grasp it and let it go, feeling every smooth area, his skin sucking itself against it. His toes felt as sensitive as fingers, touching, gripping, pushing, letting go.

As he ran, his left hand brushed the wall at his side with delicate, gentle caresses, not grasping, not pushing, not holding, his fingertips just flitting along the stone.

He held his right arm out, only slightly bent, his fingers open and spread as though to find assistance in the air itself.

Focusing his mind on the touch of his feet against the stone, he drove power down into them when he felt that he had some tiny grasp; did not force it when he felt that there was no grip, only smooth, steep stone.

He ran and ran, touching, flying, fingering, balancing, floating, as the curved wall of the funnel seemed to spin beside him.

He was trending down. He had planned to make this passage straight across the funnel from the wide ledge to the dark corridor on the other side, it, too, ending with a sharp edge at the face of the funnel.

But he was going slowly down the steep slope, each step a fraction lower than the last.

When he had left the ledge he could look across empty space and see into the dark corridor, see the small stones lying on its floor, see the walls where they touched it.

Then he could not see the floor any longer, for the opening was moving slowly, slowly upward.

If, when he reached the narrow opening of the corridor he could not get into it, all he could do was to run on, on to the edge of the funnel and then into space for there was nothing else.

The corridor was a black rectangle in the reddish-brown wall on which he ran. It was coming closer—and rising higher.

Ben flung his arms up, his fingers curled and reaching.

They found the sharp edge and locked themselves to it.

Everything stopped, the movement, the feel of air, the light touching of his feet, and he hung, his body flat against the steep wall, his arms stretched to their limits, his fingers curled over the edge of the corridor's floor.

The stone against him felt strange. It was as though, in all the time he had been running he had not been in contact with the earth, the fleeting touches of his fingers and the small areas of the soles of his feet not really touching the stone.

This stone was solid and warm and felt soft, as though he were lying on a warm, stiff-fibered carpet. It was a sleepy, delicious feeling and there was no reason to end it; just hang here on this warm carpet and sleep.

The fingers of his right hand had slipped steadily, nerve by nerve, but he had not noticed it.

Only the snapping movement of his little finger, as it slid off the edge, brought his attention to his hands and made him feel the growing strain coming down his arms in tight strings of pain.

He worked his body upward, and at last rolled over into the darkness of the narrow corridor.

His muscles trembled, jerked, shivered as he crawled on his hands and knees into what was not a corridor but a tunnel, the outer wall solidly curving over at the top and becoming a part of the butte itself.

Sometime, a million years ago when the desert was a sea, waves had formed this tunnel, wearing the sides and floor smooth, rounding the sharp edges of the stone.

Ben crawled on toward where light showed a slight bend in the tunnel. The floor here began to slope downward and was very smooth, the stone almost gleaming in the subdued light coming from the far end.

He got around the bend slowly.

And there lay the lake. A great lake of dark, sparkling, clear water, held there by the stone.

9

A CURIOUS THING has been noticed about people who are dying of thirst. The dehydration of their bodies is so extreme and the loss of salt so serious that the consistency of their blood changes radically. Sweating eventually ceases and the mucous membranes, usually moist and full of fluid, dry up and peel off. There is no saliva in their mouths or throats, and even the corners of their eyes, always flowing with moisture in normal times, become so dry that any speck of dust in their eyes causes excruciating pain.

And yet, if these people are rescued before they die, even people in the last moment of life and completely dehydrated, they almost always cry. From some mysterious storage, real tears flow from eyes that, a moment before, were bone dry and painful. No one knows where these tears come from.

Ben sat on the floor of the tunnel, his back against the curved wall of it.

It was not a lake.

It was a puddle of water about fifteen feet in

diameter and not more than two feet deep in the
deepest part. All around this puddle bird droppings had caked the floor, and the water itself
was not, as it had seemed, sparkling and clear. It
was murky and had a stale, almost dusty taste.

It was delicious.

Lying on his stomach, Ben had drunk as much
as he could. Then he had rested and drunk again.

It was as though he had actually felt this water
flowing straight through the walls of his intestines
and being taken up by his blood, and distributed
through his body.

He had drunk once more and then, asleep almost before he rolled away from the puddle, he
had lain there beside the water.

Ben felt now the way he had as a child when
he was awakened by some nightmare and his
mother had been there to comfort him. He had
never known that comfort in his uncle's house after the death of his parents. But he felt it again
now as he sat beside this little puddle, the smell of
guano strong around him.

His tongue had shrunk to its normal size, his
throat, though raw, felt good. His eyes were wet
again and he felt strength in his body.

He was hungry.

Since the first night on the low range of mountains he had not felt particularly hungry and, in
the last hours, had felt no hunger at all. But now
his stomach was gnawing at him.

The intensity of the light had changed as he
slept. Now the strongest light came from the end

of the tunnel at which he had entered and the far, unexplored end was only a dim glow.

Even his feet didn't seem to be so painful as he got up and walked around the puddle and on down the corridor.

As he neared the end he noticed where the ancient waves had worn the outer wall very thin, in places eating all the way through it so that it looked like a great slab of brownish cheese pocked with little holes.

The tunnel ended raggedly, the outer wall breaking up as the tunnel widened so that, beyond it, he could see a wide, open ledge of stone slanting upward at about 15 degrees and ending at what was apparently the top of the butte.

Ben started to walk out on the open ledge, but then for the first time in hours thought again of his enemy. Madec knew that he was somewhere on the butte. He would be waiting for just such a mistake as this.

Ben went back into the tunnel and got one of the sotol sandals. Then he knelt beside a small hole in the outer wall and slowly slid the sandal out across the opening.

No bullet ripped into it, no sound rolled up from the desert.

He tried a larger hole.

With the dark tunnel behind them these holes might look to Madec like only dark splotches on the stone surface.

He lowered the sandal and slowly moved until he could see out through the hole.

Madec was down there, sitting on the hood of the Jeep studying the butte with the binoculars, the .358 across his lap.

Ben sat down beside his puddle of water. For a long time he stared at the perfectly calm surface of it.

It was the only weapon he had; water which gave him time. If he could get some food it would add to his time, his life.

He picked up the slingshot and carried it back toward the wide end of the tunnel until he found a spot safe from Madec. There he cleared off the small pebbles and debris and sat down. He noticed as he did that his muscles were beginning to feel very stiff and painful and that, as he stooped, his back and his wounded arm ached.

It was the best slingshot he had ever seen. The handle fitted exactly into his hand, the yoke was a wide, strong U of tubular metal from the base of which the brace went down the inside of his wrist to the curved metal piece which lay against his arm, almost halfway to his elbow. There was little strain on his fingers or the palm of his hand even at full pull of the powerful rubber tubes. There was no shaking, no wavering.

Picking up a small pebble, he fitted it into the leather pouch, drew and let go. The pebble whistled out into the sunlight, hitting the wall of the butte and whining away into the air.

Gathering a little stock of pebbles, he began to shoot, aiming first at a spot close by on the wall but, as he learned to hit it with almost every try, picking targets farther and farther away, until he found the extreme range of accuracy of the slingshot.

Then, as the light slowly faded, he just sat and shot the thing, stone after stone, more and more pleased with it as his accuracy improved. He got so he could pick up a stone, pouch it, draw, shoot and hit his target with what seemed to him remarkable speed and accuracy.

At close range the slingshot was lethal. The rubber tubes were so powerful that, at full draw, Ben was sure the pebbles started out with as much velocity as the pellet of a good air gun.

Confident of his ability, he at last decided to waste one of the heavy lead buckshot, wondering what difference the smoother shape of the buckshot would make.

It made a lot.

He wasted five more of the lead bullets, finding out how much flatter their trajectory was and how much more velocity the round shape gave them.

Ready, he moved back into the tunnel, taking a position beyond the puddle so that he was almost in darkness. Arranging himself so that he would not have to move anything but his fingers drawing the pouch back, he loaded it with a buckshot and then sat, waiting.

The first bird was a sparrow hawk.

It wheeled straight into the tunnel and straight out again, banking in a sharp, whistling turn about five feet from Ben.

Discouraged, Ben sat watching the empty disk of sky he could see down the tunnel. Not a bird appeared, not even in the far distance.

Had they stopped using this water hole? Were all these droppings old? Was there water somewhere easier for them to reach?

Ben did not see them flying or see them light. They were just suddenly there, a covey of Gambel's quail walking without any hesitation into the tunnel and on toward the water.

They were talking to each other in a low, soft, fluty chatter, the little curved plumes on the heads of the males bobbing up and down as though they were nodding in agreement.

He let them come until they reached the water. Then, picking out a male standing alone, dipping his beak down and then raising it high as he let the water run down his throat, Ben drew slowly, aimed and released.

The bird dropped where he stood, a little dust of feathers settling on him and a little cloud of dust rising as he kicked feebly and then lay still.

It did not alarm the other quail at all. Some glanced at their fallen companion but did not stop drinking.

Ben eased another buckshot into the pouch, drew and shot. He did not hit this one as cleanly, apparently striking bone. The buckshot knocked the bird backward a foot or so but killed it.

He did not miss a single shot. When the birds had drunk enough they turned and walked, still chatting, out of the tunnel, leaving five dead on the floor.

He gathered them up and took them to the funnel end where there was more light. They were still warm as he plucked them, the feathers remarkably hard to pull out.

The little carcasses looked pitiful, as they lay in a row on the rock, the heads unplucked, the gay plumes limp now and colorless.

Ben tried not to look at them as he gouged them open with his thumbnail, their juices covering his hands. He debated about throwing the entrails away but at last did, thinking that other quail would be back for water in the morning.

Ben looked at the raw, bloody thing in his fingers, the bones showing ghastly white in what was left of the sunset.

Then, and with his eyes shut, gagging, he put it to his mouth and tore the flesh off with his teeth. Close to nausea, he did not chew at all, just swallowed the tough, slimy stuff, forcing his throat to accept it.

He ate them all, the process getting no easier. When they were all gone he looked at his hands, dark with blood, and felt the blood around his mouth and almost lost the meal.

I can't go on doing that, Ben decided.

If the birds came back in the morning he would dress them out and then put them in the sun. No matter how hungry he felt he would make himself wait until the sun on the stone had cooked them—at least a little.

His mind went on, dealing only with small things, not wanting to deal with the one enormous thing which, as he slowly admitted it into his thoughts, was like the darkness creeping up the side of the butte and into the tunnel.

10

THERE WERE VOICES in the wind. Off and on all night Ben had listened to them: the whispering, the faint dry laughter, the chattering that sometimes sounded insane. As a little boy he had heard these wind voices and they had scared him, but his father had told him that the desert had to talk at night. That it was so silent during the day it just had to break out into all this talk at night.

Ben had never been afraid of the voices after that.

He had slept all night, guarded against Madec by birds that had come at sunset to roost at the mouth of the tunnel. Every time Ben moved in his sleep they fluttered and cried out, hustling away from him.

At dawn he had shot six birds, using only pebbles in the slingshot, saving the buckshot for a time when he might need the greater velocity and greater accuracy. He had plucked and cleaned them more efficiently than he had the others and now they were lying out on a smooth, clean rock, the sun already beginning to cook them.

Using water from the puddle, he had cleaned all the wounds he could reach and was pleased to see how fast they were healing. He had inspected his slingshot, examining the rubber tubes carefully to see that they were not beginning to break or wear at any place.

His beard was now six days old, for he made it a practice not to shave during long trips in the desert; a beard helped protect his face from the sun. When he looked at himself in the surface of the water his beard was very black and thick and gave him a strange, Satanic look; he looked dangerous.

Ben had a pleasant sense of well-being as he sat down in the tunnel out of reach of Madec's gun and started practicing with the slingshot. His wounds only hurt when he moved carelessly, his arm only ached a little and, although he was hungry, he was content to wait until the carcasses became more appetizing.

He was getting so good with the slingshot that he could hit within an inch of where he aimed at thirty feet. At fifteen feet he was accurate even with a stone.

A nine-inch whiptail lizard came into view, and Ben threw a pebble at it to get it moving and then nailed it on the run at twenty feet.

He added it to his cooking birds and then stopped for a moment and looked through his peekhole at Madec.

The man had pitched camp at the foot of the

butte, getting the Jeep in close to the breccia. He had parked facing the butte and had put up the tent behind the Jeep. The water cans were in under the awning of the tent, lined up in a neat row in the shade.

Madec was doing something around behind the Jeep. Ben could see his shadow moving.

As he sat down again and fitted the slingshot back into his hand he knew that it was foolish to imagine that he was safe just because he had food and water and Madec could not shoot him.

Madec would change that.

He was locked to that man down on the desert. They were chained together.

Perhaps a different man would have left the desert by now, sure that Ben could not make it out. But Madec would not do that. He would stay until he saw that his plan had been worked out to the last detail.

Madec would not leave him here alive.

As Ben sat going over in his mind what had happened since the first roar of that .358, a thought formed and became clearer and clearer until he realized that it was the only thing he could do.

The chain between them was hundreds of feet long now, stretching from high on the butte down the steep side, across the breccia and the smoother, sandier desert and over to the Jeep, locking at last to Madec.

For me to live, Ben thought, that chain must

be drawn shorter. It must be drawn in link by link until he and I are face to face.

And somehow when we do come face to face, he must be as naked as I am.

I cannot let Madec come to me, Ben thought. I cannot let him choose his place and his time and his method of coming.

I must either go to him or I must pull him to me.

Ben laid aside the slingshot and went over to a hole in the wall.

Madec was walking toward the butte.

He had the big gun slung over one shoulder and the coil of tow rope over the other and was carrying the heavy canvas bag in which Ben stowed tools and gear.

He's coming to me, Ben thought. Coming at his choice of place and time and method.

Madec disappeared from view as he moved in close to the wall of the butte.

Ben went on to the end of the tunnel and waited there, not exposing himself.

The sound was clear but faint. Listening to it he could almost see what Madec was doing down there.

In the canvas bag there was a geological hammer with a flat peen on one end and a long, rock-breaking spike on the other. Madec was down there at the foot of the butte cutting a stairway up the side of it.

The sound ceased for a moment and then a new sound came up, clear and almost musical, the sound of metal hammering metal.

Now he was driving a piton into a crack in the rock.

For a moment Ben wondered what Madec was using for a piton. Then he thought of the long steel pegs he carried in case he had to pitch a tent in stony ground with a high wind.

With the rope secured to the tent pegs driven into the face of the wall and with handholds and footholds hacked out of it, Madec was starting to climb the butte.

Although he knew that Madec probably could not see him, Ben took no chances as he left the tunnel and went out on the wide ledge. Staying low against the far side, which rose in a smooth wall, he hurried along, noticing as he went how the ledge not only slanted upward but was narrowing.

At last the ledge became so narrow that he could not walk on it and, a few feet farther on, faired back into the escarpment.

The escarpment was a wall of smooth stone, inclined outward. This leaning wall towered above him for more than fifty feet and formed, it appeared, the top of the butte.

About twenty feet beyond where he stood, but above him, was another ledge, wide and slanting upward; an easy path to the top of the butte.

No force in the world would hold him against that leaning wall long enough to cross those twenty feet to the wide avenue of stone going to the top.

Nor was there any way a naked man with no tools could scale the escarpment.

He was confined to this narrow ledge and the tunnel. He was imprisoned here.

And Madec knew that.

Ben could now see exactly what Madec was planning. About where Madec was, Ben remembered, there was a smooth, unclimbable wall from the breccia to a ledge about thirty feet up.

Ben had studied this place longingly, for once on that high ledge it had looked to him as though the rest of the way to the top would be no more than a stiff walk. Without tools and rope he hadn't been able to conquer the first, smooth, vertical obstacle.

Madec had everything he needed.

Ben studied the stone butte, from where Madec would start on the first ledge to where he would end at the top.

Wherever Madec would be in sight he would be out of range of the slingshot.

And at those same places Ben would be an easy target for the gun.

He realized slowly and bitterly that he could not stop Madec from climbing. He could not even harass him and slow him down.

Ben looked across at the ledge twenty feet above him. He studied it for a moment and then slowly looked back along his own ledge and on into the deep shadows of the tunnel.

From the wide ledge toward which he was climbing Madec could stand—or even sit comfortably, his elbows wedged down against his legs for firm support—and shoot him.

Ben could see from one end of the dark tunnel to the other. Not even the bend in the tunnel was enough to conceal him.

There was no place to hide.

Ben went back along the ledge and into the tunnel to where the slingshot lay beside the little pile of stones he had gathered.

The sound of the hammer seemed to beat against him as he sat beside the slingshot and idly fitted it into his hand.

Ben was listening so intently to the hammer that it was a long time before he realized he had also been hearing the sound above him.

It was a hollow, rattling, irritating noise. He ran to the mouth of the tunnel and looked up.

The helicopter was like transparent gold floating in the sky, coming nearer and nearer.

He could not make out the markings on it, but he was sure that it was the Game and Fish chopper on a routine patrol.

It was the most beautiful thing Ben had ever seen in his life.

BEN COULDN'T BE SURE, but when the chopper went into a sharp skid and floated gently to the ground not a hundred feet from the Jeep, he would have bet money that Denny O'Neil was flying it.

Ben felt so good he was jumping up and down on the ledge, yelling his lungs out as the dust of the chopper's landing blew away and he saw a man get out of it and run, stooped, out from under the rotors.

He had expected to see a game warden and had hoped that it would be the supervisor, Les Stanton, but the man was in civilian clothes.

Ben calmed down, saving his breath and waiting for the chopper blades to stop but, as he waited, he realized that although the engine had slowed and the blades were just lazily turning, it hadn't stopped.

It wasn't going to stop. Not if Denny O'Neil were flying it. Denny had told him once, "Ben, the trouble with you is that you think engines *want* to run. Well, I got news for you—they don't.

Any time they can get away with not running, believe me, they'll do it. And engines are smart. And they're mean. When everything's going good up in that chopper and you can see forever, that engine'll run, but you get in trouble in bad weather and get down in a gorge you *got* to *fly* out of and that engine'll quit. Engines don't like people and you better believe it.

"Out there on the desert," Denny had told him, "in that chopper, I know that engine's just waiting for me to get myself in a bind so it can quit. Well, I don't let it. I start that booger up in the morning, and I don't let it quit until I'm home again."

Ben went to the edge of the cliff, cupped his hands around his mouth and yelled as loudly as he could. He kept on yelling and moving, jumping, swaying, waving his arms.

Denny O'Neil didn't get out of the chopper. The other man walked over to Madec, who was now beside the Jeep, and Ben watched them as they talked.

They probably had to yell at each other to be heard over the sound of the engine.

The man looked like Les Stanton, but he had on a purple shirt outside his yellow trousers and he wasn't wearing a hat.

When Ben saw the man's shoes he knew it wasn't Les. Les wouldn't be caught dead in the desert in a pair of low-cut white shoes.

Still trying to attract their attention, Ben could feel something dying inside him.

This was where Madec would be good. His lies would be smooth, logical and convincing.

The man shook hands with Madec and went back to the chopper.

Still yelling and knowing that it was useless, Ben watched the chopper swirl up, emerge from its cloud of dust and go away.

It disappeared so fast, so fast, leaving only the fading sound of Denny's always running engine to taunt him for a moment longer.

Ben walked slowly into the tunnel and stood at one of the biggest of the water-worn holes looking down.

Madec was walking briskly back toward the butte.

Ben watched him until he was out of sight under the overhang. For a long time he just stood there, defeated, listening to the hammer, hoping the chopper would come back, but knowing that it would not.

Then, finally, he wandered out of the tunnel, out onto the ledge and along it to the end. There he leaned out as far as he could, keeping one hand firmly on the cliff face, and looked down.

Whatever Madec did he did well. He was braced now, the rope around his waist, about fifteen feet above the ground, his boots firmly planted in the footholds he had chopped out, the rope secured around a tent peg driven into a crack in the rock.

He was chopping a new handhold, the hammer head glinting in the sunlight.

It would take Madec the rest of the day to chop his way up to the first ledge. From there the rest was just a stroll up the butte, no problem.

Madec wouldn't come up there at night. He was too cautious to do that.

He would finish cutting his little holes in the rock and finish driving his spikes where he needed them and then, when all was ready, he would wait out the night and come in the morning.

Returning to the tunnel, Ben looked out through its stone mouth, which seemed to frame a picture and make it more vivid.

The far mountains were masses of purple, rugged and alive looking. These were not the old, worn, tree-covered mountains he had seen in other places. These were tough, young mountains, their peaks sharp and strong against the deep blue of the sky, their ridges full of vigor.

And the desert itself was not the bleak and arid place it seemed, but a place full of life. A place where a plant might lie dormant for years and then, with the first drops of rain, spring to full life, produce its flowers, cast its seed and die—all in twenty-four hours.

The hammer had stopped.

It was insulting; the thought of being killed here in the desert where he had always lived by this man from the city was insulting and outrageous.

Ben got to his feet slowly and walked down to the narrow end of the tunnel. As he did so, he made his decision.

Ben sat on the edge of the stone, his feet hanging down in the bisected funnel and leaned over, looking down at the steep, smooth surface of the funnel, studying it down and down until the top of the funnel spout, also bisected, narrowed sharply, going straight on down to the breccia. He noted every wrinkle in it, every rough patch, every stratum. He studied each change in the basalt's texture and memorized every tiny fissure in the surface of the stone.

After an hour he got up and went back to the other end of the ledge. There, not exposing himself, he stood and looked down at the desert, his eyes ranging from the jumble of rock at the base of the butte out across a sandy area and then into a harder, rock-strewn stretch where the Jeep was parked.

During a few seconds in, perhaps, ten million years a slab of the butte had cracked off. Shaken by an earthquake or moved by the force of some great wind or shrunk by cold, the slab had fallen, one enormous solid slab of stone.

When it had hit the desert, it had broken all to pieces.

One piece, as big as a pickup truck, had apparently bounced or rolled out beyond the breccia and lay isolated on the floor of the desert.

Madec, going back and forth between the butte and the slab of stone, had skirted it, his tracks a clear path around one end.

Ben looked down at these tracks and at that

great chunk of stone for a long time and then carefully searched the other areas.

There were no other tracks, only those leading from the Jeep, around the slab, and onto the butte.

Judging from the mark of Madec's feet, just traces on the hard surface, but deep prints in the sand, and almost invisible in the breccia, it looked to Ben as though the wind had piled up four or five feet of blow sand all around the slab.

Going back again to the narrow end of the tunnel, he resumed his study, noting now the position of the slab in relation to the spout of the funnel and the camp Madec had made around the Jeep.

The position, Ben decided, was very good.

The sun was setting now and Madec, evidently finished for the day, appeared walking back to the Jeep.

Ben sat there studying him, studying every step he took and what effort he had to exert to take it.

Madec carried the rope coiled on his shoulder; the canvas bag was in his hand; two canteens bounced on his hips; and the gun was cradled in his arm.

He walked where he had walked before, going around the eastern end of the slab and on toward the Jeep.

Ben watched some Gambel's quail strolling into the tunnel for their evening drink. He did not move as they dipped and raised their heads, murmuring to each other. The slingshot lay gleaming dully in the fading light but he did not reach for it.

The birds wandered out again and then, as though recess was over, gathered in an almost military fashion and suddenly, all together, took off in a small, soft explosion of wings.

Ben picked up the slingshot and began working with it. Strips of tough leather with slots in the ends held the rubber tubes to the yoke and pouch. It was easy to slide the leather back through the slots and release both ends of the tubes.

The hollow in the tubes was about three-eighths of an inch in diameter, the rubber a thick wall around it.

He blew through both tubes and then laid them down on the stone.

Putting the four little leather thongs and the leather shot-holder into the bullet pouch, he drew the drawstring tight and tied it to a sotol fiber.

With another fiber he bound the rubber tubes to the yoke and tied the yoke to the first fiber. Then, as the last light died, he strung four fibers together into a stout cord and tied the slingshot and pouch to it, putting the loop of it over his head so that his little kit of equipment hung down on his chest.

In the dark now, he went to the far end of the tunnel, got the still-warm carcasses of the birds and the lizard and, forcing himself not to think about it, sat beside the water and ate them all, pulling the meat of the lizard away from the tough, sandy-feeling skin with his teeth.

Finished, he leaned down to the water and drank. He kept on drinking long after he had reached his fill, drinking until he ached.

Then, his naked body ghostly in the dark tunnel, he went back to the funnel and sat down, his feet dangling.

The Coleman lantern below on the desert seemed very bright, a hard, white, unblinking light. Occasionally he could see Madec as he moved around.

Madec, Ben said in a whisper, you're tired. You've done a bang-up job today; you've worked hard and lied well. You deserve a good night's rest. You *need* a good night's rest because you've got a big thing to do in the morning.

Ben saw the Coleman moving under the tent awning and into the tent and then the entire tent glowed.

At last the glow faded and suddenly died.

Ben never took his eyes off the camp which, almost invisible at first with the Coleman out, slowly began to take shape again in the starlight. He saw no movement and was sure, as time passed, that Madec was still in the tent. Asleep by now, he hoped.

He had decided that it was time when he suddenly jumped up and went back into the tunnel.

Feeling around among the bird droppings, he found the last of his sotol leaves and, as he walked back to the funnel, tore it into four wide strips.

Sitting down again, he slipped the yoke over his head and strung the torn leaf to it, pushing the strips down until they hung with the sling-shot and pouch.

Now it was time. He turned, his legs sliding down, his back to the stone and eased himself over the edge until he was hanging by his hands, his toes on the stone slope below. Then he let go.

12

HIS SPEED in the darkness was terrifying. Lying on his back now, he slid feet first down the steep stone funnel.

He had thought that even in the dark he would recognize the features in the stone, and would know, feeling one, where the next rough spot would be.

But his hands and skin and heels and back recognized nothing as he skidded downward, the hard rock flaying him.

Along with the terror of his speed there was the knowledge that he could not stop, could not even slow the rate at which he was moving. Worst of all he could not see where he was going. He could see only the rushing stone face opposite him and the star-pricked sky.

The slingshot yoke tinkled on the stone and the sotol brushed dryly on it, and his own body, sliding, made a dry, rushing sound, and he could feel patches of blow sand as hot as coals grinding into his skin.

His feet hit the top opening of the spout, jamming his legs back, folding them at the knees, before skidding on down.

Then he was entirely in the spout of the funnel, his feet flat against one side, his buttocks and back against the other.

He slid in this position for ten more feet before he could stop himself.

Then he sat suspended, the friction of his feet and back the only things holding him from falling on down the long, dark, narrow spout of rock.

Leaning toward his bent knees until he could feel that the loss of pressure on his back was getting dangerous, Ben looked down between his legs.

He could make it if he wasn't careless.

Ben had no idea how long it took him to get down to the desert but, at last, he stood in the shadow of the butte, his muscles slowly relaxing, his breathing slowing, his pain coming down from a high scream to a sharp ache.

In the moonlight the camp seemed far away and very still, nothing moving anywhere.

And suddenly Ben began to doubt himself. Standing there, only a few minutes' easy walk to where Madec lay sleeping, was different from being up there in the tunnel. Up there the first and biggest problem had been simply to get down.

Now, with the tent and Jeep in clear view, he began to wonder whether the plan he had so carefully made on the butte was really the best thing to do.

That plan was so slow, so time-consuming and dangerous.

Wouldn't it be simpler and less dangerous just to walk quietly over to the camp, pick the Hornet out of the scabbard on the windshield and walk into the tent, shoving the muzzle of the Hornet in Madec's face as he woke up?

Unless Madec heard or saw him coming and was waiting in the dark, and the big gun blasted him before he even reached the Jeep.

Or wouldn't it be a better idea to wait, hidden by that solitary slab of stone, until Madec came to the butte in the morning and, as he passed, nail him with the slingshot?

But what if Madec just happened to choose a different route?

Or, Ben thought, now that I've got forty-eight hours of water in my belly, why not just take off for home? Go as far as I can until the sun begins to hurt me, hide and then start out again after sunset.

Hide—where? Go—on what? Forty-five miles on sotol leaves?

No. The plan he had made on the butte was a good plan. Slow, yes, but careful. And with danger reduced to only one thing: the .358.

Moving along beside the base of the butte, Ben deliberately stepped on the flattest, grayest stones he could see and, having stepped on them, stooped and looked at where he had stepped. He knew his back was bloody from the grinding on the rock, but apparently there were no serious gashes in his skin, for he was leaving no sign of blood on the stones, and as he went on he could almost feel the desert air drying the blood on his back, forming a layer of dried blood which seemed to pull gently at his nerve ends.

Moving slowly and keeping out of sight of the camp he followed the base of the butte around to where he could see Madec's tent pegs and footholds in the sheer wall.

Here he turned and looked out at the slab of stone imbedded in the sand. It lay about halfway between the butte and the Jeep and completely blocked his view of the camp.

Ben found some consolation in knowing that the slab also blocked Madec's view.

Reaching around behind his back, he tore the sotol strips loose and bundled the ends in his hands.

Ready, he started walking toward the Jeep along the path Madec had made.

Ben walked backward and stooped over, stopping frequently to look toward the Jeep and to listen, and, as he walked, brushing his tracks with the leaves as he made them. He didn't try to brush them out entirely but only to blur them so that the prints of his bare feet didn't lie like signals on top of the boot prints below them.

The passage between the butte and the slab took longer than he had expected. It worried him, for he had much to do, and it could only be done while Madec slept.

Reaching the slab at last, he left Madec's path and, ignoring the tracks he was making in the deep, soft sand, went along the slab, the great gray mass of it between him and the Jeep.

Halfway along it he stopped and dropped to his knees.

It was good sand, loose, dry—and deep. There would be no problem.

He went back to the path and, again walking backward, completely erased the footprints he had made alongside the slab, hating the time it took but knowing that he must do it and do it carefully and well.

Then, at the end of the slab farthest from Madec's tracks, he began to dig, using his hands like a scoop and piling the sand carefully beside the hole.

After a while he tested the hole, found it too shallow, and dug some more until it was deep enough.

Standing in the hole he had dug, he reached out with the strips of leaves and erased every mark he had made around it, wishing all the time that the dry sotol leaves would not make so much noise.

Finished, he laid the strips carefully in the hole and then pulled the yoke over his head.

He untied the rubber tubes from the slingshot and then laid the slingshot and pouch, still on the yoke, down in the hole on the left side.

He was ready now and yet he hesitated, unable

to overcome the feeling of terror which suddenly struck him, making him literally sick.

He had to force himself to do it, but at last he got down in the hole and slowly rolled over until he was lying on his back in the bottom of the grave-shaped hole in the sand of the desert.

The slingshot pressed against him and was uncomfortable so he moved it away an inch and then, sitting up, began to scoop the sand in over himself, starting at his feet and working on up his legs.

When he could no longer do it sitting up, he lay back down again and pulled the warm, dry stuff in on top of himself, up his belly, across his chest, up until he felt it dry and gritty in the hairs of his beard.

He stopped then and got the two slingshot rubbers.

With his left hand he fitted one end of one of the rubbers in his left ear. When it was well in, he held it there with his left hand as he carefully scooped sand in around the left side of his head and ear. He continued scooping, moving his fingers slowly up the tube, keeping it erect, until the sand was at the level of his eyes.

Then he took the other tube in his right hand and put one end in his mouth. Holding it there with his teeth, he swung it over a little until his left hand was holding both tubes upright.

Moving his head, he got his chin down on his chest, the tubes still in his ear and mouth, so that his nose would not be clogged too badly.

Ben looked up once again at the clear, high sky. The moon had set and the stars were dimming.

Ben closed his eyes and with his right hand began to pull the sand down on his head, up around his right ear and on, the sand rolling in tiny waves of dryness across his face, covering his eyes, nose and forehead.

When he was sure that the two tubes were firmly held in place by the sand, he turned them loose with his left hand and worked his hand and arm down below the sand until it lay along his side.

With his right hand he kept on pulling the sand over him, feeling occasionally with his fingers for the tube ends.

When there was only an inch or so of the tubing above the level of the sand he stopped, suddenly panicked. If he left that much tube exposed, Madec could easily see it. On the other hand, if he piled sand right up to the tube openings, hiding all sign of them, it would not take much of a wind to start sand blowing across them.

Then sand would come down the tube in his ear and cut off his only contact with the outside world. Worse, that windblown sand could cut off his air and force him to push his head up into full view.

Fighting the panic, Ben again began moving the sand very carefully, piling it up around the tubes in a little mound. That way, he hoped, they would be hidden and at the same time the wind would not blow sand down into them.

With the tubes set, he brushed blindly and for as far as he could reach across the sand covering him, hoping he was leaving it so that Madec would not notice that it had been disturbed.

At last, putting his right arm at full length beside his body, he began working it gently downward.

When his right arm was down alongside him, he realized that there was nothing he could do about the mark it had left on the surface of the sand. He could only hope that it was a confused, indistinct sand formation which would tell Madec nothing if he happened to glance over at it on his way to the butte.

For a time—he did not know how long—Ben was so concentrated on the small things that there was no room for the horror.

First it was the tube in his mouth. Although he had been breathing through it for some time, he suddenly began to think about it, to wonder if he could keep on breathing through it, for as many hours as it took.

It required no effort. The air came down easily and went out easily, and he had only to remember not to breathe in or out through his nose.

Next he worried that he could hear nothing through the tube in his ear. It was as though the whole world had gone dead silent.

If he could not hear, all this was useless and he might as well be buried in his grave. Hearing was his only contact with Madec.

All his senses seemed to concentrate in his left

ear, trying to force some sound to come down the tube.

And then he thought in terror, Is the tube plugged?

He fought the panic which had now taken shape and become a force he could feel coiling under him like springs that would soon release and hurl him straight up out of there.

Drawing in a deep breath, he held it for a second and then forced it whistling out of the tube.

The sound it made at the other end was sharp and distinct.

He felt the sand move as his body relaxed with pure relief.

Then he recognized this new danger and began to feel with each breath how much the sand was moving on his body.

The panic swept over him again in wave after wave of blind terror.

This is my grave. I'm in my grave. I'm buried alive.

He couldn't control it and, as though it had no connection with him, he heard his breath whistling and gasping in the tube. When he could think at all, it was only that he was lying buried here, totally at Madec's mercy.

The horror never again left him, but he made himself breathe shallowly, made his stomach stop the wild, panicked heaving.

Gradually, he realized that the air he was breathing was warmer. The sun must be high now, the day well along.

Where was Madec? What was he doing?

Had he already gone by? Was he now at the butte, perhaps already climbing it?

If Madec had already gone to the butte he would climb it and, when he found Ben gone, would first search the desert with his binoculars and, not finding him, would begin to search the ground for tracks. . . .

Ben felt the grave closing in on him again.

The sotol leaf . . . a green thing where nothing was green. A leaf evidently torn apart by a man's hands.

Was it lying out there on the sand?

Stupid. Stupid. Stupid.

No. He had buried it. . . . someone was talking. There were voices. . . .

Far away and wordless, but voices. Like the thin sound of television at a long distance. A flat, high-pitched sound.

It was the radio in the Jeep.

The voices changed to music and then abruptly stopped, leaving Ben in silence.

It won't be long now, Ben thought, hearing his own breath coming out of the tube.

He breathed more gently and slowly until there was only a whisper of sound.

There was a dull, indistinct clanking sound coming from somewhere, and as Ben listened, he realized that sounds coming through the tube had no direction; they seemed to originate in the tube itself.

That clanking sound could have come from

the butte—Madec driving a spike—or it could have come from the Jeep.

In the short time since the radio had been turned off Madec could not have reached the butte.

Ben realized he must analyze any sound he heard by the sound alone, for there would be no direction, no point of origin to help him.

He was tired now, the effort of concentration and his fear were draining him.

Come on, Madec! he thought. *Come on!*

13

IT WOULD BE so easy for Madec to kill him, Ben thought.

If Madec noticed his tracks in the path, or if the sand where he was buried was disturbed enough to attract his attention or if he just happened to see the two little tubes sticking up out of the sand, it would be a simple thing for him to walk over to Ben's grave, stand on top of it and put his finger on the end of the tube. With the weight of Madec added to the weight of the sand on top of him, his arms pinned to his sides, he would be helpless and, in two or three minutes, he would be dead.

This was a disaster, and too much time had now passed for him to correct it. He could not move now; could not spring up from the sand and escape. He was trapped here, as though Madec himself had planned this thing.

Ben couldn't tell from which direction the steps were coming. There was no way to distinguish that. But they were coming. They were only soft whispers of sound at first, but now he could distinctly hear Madec's hard-soled boots on the small rocks.

The sound stopped.

He is standing there, Ben thought in terror. He's seen something and stopped walking.

There was a faint, unrecognizable sound in the tube for a second and then silence again.

Had it been Madec taking the rifle off his shoulder? Or putting the tool bag and rope down?

He heard the sound again, but it was so soft and so indistinct that he could not even guess what was making it.

And then he felt a movement, the sand around his body seeming to compress slightly.

Madec is coming toward me, Ben thought. He's seen the tubes and is coming.

He thought of pulling the tubes down below the sand and then realized that in itself would kill him and, to do it, he would have to move an arm —which would also get him killed.

He was absolutely helpless.

The almost imperceptible compression of the sand continued—coming, Ben thought, in quick, spaced waves.

And then there was no more movement.

Is he standing there, looking down at the tubes?

What is Madec doing? Why is he taking so long?

As though in answer Ben heard a faint and apparently faraway *chink*. A tiny metallic *chink*.

He heard it again and then again.

Madec was hammering on something.

Ben listened, concentrated.

He was hammering not on rock but on metal.

Unless the man completely understood the passage of sound down the tube; unless he knew that it came to Ben without direction and was so distorted as to be hard to identify, then he was at the base of the butte, hammering his spikes in the wall.

But if Madec did understand, he could be standing within two feet of Ben and simply clicking the sling ring against the barrel of the rifle.

How would he know what sound would be like coming down a tube directly into your ear?

I don't think he knows that, Ben decided.

Pushing with his arms and the muscles of his shoulders and neck, he forced his head slowly up through the heavy sand, inching up until his elbows were under his back.

When his head was out of the sand he shook it only enough to clear the sand from his eyes and then opened them.

Madec was almost to the top of the sheer wall, the wide ledge going up to the top of the butte only a few feet above him. He was standing in a foothold he had cut. The rope around his waist was attached to a tent peg he had driven into the wall just above his head.

He looked like some huge, distorted fly clinging to the rock as he leaned back, methodically chipping away.

Ben got out of the grave as fast as he could and began pushing the sand back into it.

He had almost covered the rubberless yoke of the slingshot, when he changed his mind and fished it out.

He smoothed the sand hurriedly and then tried to make only indistinct footprints as he went over to Madec's path.

Once behind the slab he began to run toward the Jeep.

As he ran he wondered where Madec's gun was, trying to remember if Madec had it slung over his shoulder. He could not remember seeing it at all.

Perhaps Madec, not yet ready to climb the butte, felt so secure that he had not even taken the gun with him. Perhaps it was there in the Jeep with the Hornet.

Ben brushed the hope aside, not wanting it to cloud anything.

That gun was what he must concentrate on first. As long as Madec had the gun Ben could not draw him close, could not control him. But once he had the gun . . .

He was still fifteen feet from the Jeep when he saw the beat-up stock of the Hornet sticking out of the steel scabbard below the windshield.

The sight of it made him feel good. He loved that old, obsolete gun he had had ever since he was a kid. These modern guns were hotter, with more velocity, flatter trajectories, and greater accuracy, but Ben knew to the fraction of an inch what that old Hornet would do—and wouldn't do—and it was all the gun he had ever needed.

He streaked around behind the Jeep and there, concealed from Madec, crouched and looked over the back.

Madec was still hammering away at the wall.

The big .358 Winchester was on the ground below Madec, standing propped against the wall. The underside of the gun was toward Ben, the metal of the trigger guard black against the polished, light-tan wood of the stock.

Ben was sure that with one, or at most two, shots from the Hornet he could put the big gun out of commission. He would aim first at the trigger guard, hoping to smash it in and jam the trigger, but if that didn't do it, he could tear the gun up, jamming the clip, ruining the scope, perhaps even blasting the action loose, before Madec could get down off the wall.

Still crouched, Ben sneaked along the side of the Jeep and, just reaching up with his hand, got a grip on the Hornet and pulled it slowly out of the scabbard.

Going back to the rear so that he could crouch there, the barrel of the gun out along the can rack, Ben got down into position, slowly pushed the gun out, and took a preliminary look through the scope.

The four-power glass brought the trigger guard leaping toward him.

Fish in a barrel, he thought. He reached automatically for the knob of the bolt to check that a cartridge was chambered.

There was no knob. . . .

There was no bolt.

Ben looked down where it should have been and could see the top cartridge in the clip, the brass case shiny and new, the brass-jacketed bullet a duller color.

Without the bolt the gun and cartridges were useless. A metal tube, little containers of gun powder, a magnifying glass.

Ben moved forward along the Jeep until he could reach into the glove compartment and feel around, identifying things with his fingers—the rubber snake-bite kit, papers, a packet of matches, a pair of gloves, a plastic case for his sunglasses.

The bolt for the rifle was not there.

He had to risk being seen as he got into the Jeep and, watching Madec when he could, searched it.

The bolt was not in it.

Crouched in the Jeep, his head just high enough to look out through the windshield, he stared at Madec's gun leaning there against the stone, the sun hot on it.

Could he run fast enough to get the gun before Madec could come down off the cliff face?

No. A loop of rope around one of the tent pegs reached all the way to the ground. Madec could come down that rope in a matter of seconds and be standing there, gun in hand, as Ben came panting up.

For a moment he slumped in the driver's seat, out of sight of Madec, and felt like crying.

Then slowly, he began to realize that it was not

the missing bolt of the Hornet that was defeating
him. It was that man hammering on the wall of
the butte.

Madec.

And Ben realized that, for the last few minutes, he had not even been thinking about Madec.

In the mountains and on the butte he had felt
that he was locked to Madec, that he could not
leave him. And this had made everything he did
complicated and dangerous.

Now, in the Jeep, everything was simple.

He was no longer chained to Madec.

All he had to do was drive back to town and
go to the sheriff.

The whole operation would take six, maybe
seven hours. He and the sheriff would be back
out here in the chopper before sunset.

Madec, on foot, wouldn't even be really tired
when they picked him up.

Ben pushed up in the seat high enough to look
at Madec, who was now doing something with the
rope.

Suddenly Ben relaxed, realizing that he had all
the time in the world.

Madec still had work to do before he reached
the first ledge. That would take time. Before he
went up on the ledge, he'd have to come down
and get the gun. Then he would have to climb
back up.

The time to go would be when Madec reached

the top of the butte and was searching for him down in the tunnel.

Ben looked out across the desert, picking his track. For at least a mile he could keep the Jeep in two-wheel drive. The ground here was firm enough to let him really gun it at the start and in seconds he'd be going thirty or forty miles an hour.

With any luck he'd be out of range of the big gun before Madec even reacted to the sound of the engine.

He sat for a moment longer just enjoying this sudden feeling of freedom. The chain linking him and the man on the stone wall was broken.

Ben grinned as he decided it might look better if he didn't drive into town naked. Rolling out of the Jeep, he crawled around to the rear. There were no clothes in the Jeep so he went on to the tent.

Madec made a neat, orderly camp, his cooking fire still smoldering a little in its ring of rocks, all the water and rations in out of the sun. Inside the tent the sight of Madec's sleeping bag almost made Ben laugh out loud. It was neatly rolled and stowed in the tote bag.

You didn't think you'd need it for another night, did you, Madec? Ben thought.

Well, you won't. They've got a real bed for you in the jail.

Madec's leather suitcase was locked, and the heavy canvas duffel bag was closed at the throat by a thin metal cable and was also locked.

There was no sign of his, or the old man's, clothes, and Ben guessed that he had them out of sight in the duffel.

There'd be plenty of time later on to get the duffel open, he thought. Leaving the suitcase and sleeping bag and Coleman lantern in the tent, he loaded the duffel bag, water and food into the back of the Jeep.

Ready now, he slid back into the driver's seat and looked again at Madec on the wall. The man had almost reached the ledge.

Idly, Ben felt for the ignition key.

Somehow he was not surprised when his fingers found that the key was gone.

That's what a dude from the city would do, Ben thought. Take the keys out—with a car a million miles from nowhere in the middle of the desert.

Probably had the key in his pocket, the idiot.

No problem. Hot-wiring a Jeep was only a matter of yanking the left-hand wire off the switch and wrapping it around the right-hand post.

He was reaching under the dash to do this when he glanced at Madec again.

The man wasn't doing anything. He was just hanging in his rope sling, looking up as though studying what his next move would be.

The silence worried Ben a little. This was a brand-new Jeep—he remembered the trouble he'd had starting it when he went up to get the old man—and Madec had bounced it around some more since then.

No use taking a chance on a loose wire. Once he snapped that hot wire on the post the Jeep would have to *move*.

Madec was hammering again as Ben, on his hands and knees, crawled around the Jeep unlatching first one side of the hood and then the other and lifting it just enough to get his hands underneath.

The first thing he touched was the top of the distributor cap.

The black plastic felt warm and oily.

It was lying loose on the plug wire harness.

The rotor was gone, the mortised metal shaft sticking up like something naked.

Ben slowly withdrew his hand and let the hood down.

Numb, he crawled around to the back of the Jeep and sat down. He knew that he should be searching for the rotor, should be breaking open that suitcase and the duffel bag, he should be rooting in the food cans and fishing in the water cans, should be under the Jeep where Madec might have taped both the rotor and the Hornet bolt.

But he just sat there, knowing that no searching would do any good. The key, the bolt, and the rotor were in Madec's pocket or in the tool bag Ben had seen on the ground at the butte.

Madec's hammering sounded almost gay, a

steady tinkling beat in the silence.

The chain between them was there again; he and Madec were, again, locked together.

The feeling that he had had in the tunnel came slowly back. He, not Madec, must gather in that chain. He must draw Madec to him, closer and closer until at last he could reach out with his hand and touch him.

Ben picked up the slingshot yoke where he had dropped it on the sand and then found the two rubber tubes, still lying on the tailgate.

Getting the leather thongs out of the bullet pouch, he strung the tubes in place and tested them, drawing the empty holder back to his chin.

Standing up, but concealed by the Jeep, he studied the ground between him and the butte.

He could not go to Madec, could not risk being seen out there on the open desert. With the Hornet he could have done it, holding Madec on the wall with the gun. But the slingshot could not do that.

Madec would have to come to him.

One toot on the Jeep's horn would accomplish that—in a hurry.

But he would gain nothing if he made Madec come to him armed and ready to shoot.

He must come to me carelessly, Ben thought. He must come feeling safe and unthreatened.

Opening the leather pouch, he emptied a dozen of the buckshot out on the white, flat surface of the open tailgate and then lined them up carefully with his finger so that each one lay about an inch from the others. Then he put the slingshot down and reached into the glove compartment.

Watching Madec as he moved, he went into the tent and unzipped the tote bag.

He felt a little twinge of regret as he pulled out Madec's sleeping bag. It was a beauty, all soft nylon and goose down; it had probably cost Madec more than a hundred dollars.

He unrolled it, pushing it close to the tent wall and then threw the tote bag over against the other wall.

He unhooked the Coleman lantern, glad, for once, that Madec was such a methodical man. There was no sloshing around in the fuel tank.

Unscrewing the filler cap, Ben doused the sleeping bag and the tote bag with the ninety octan white gas and then dumped the last few ounces on the ground cover.

He started to put the lantern down on the floor but then carefully screwed the cap back on it and dropped it on the sleeping bag.

He waited until he was well outside and under the awning before he lit the match and flicked it in on the sleeping bag.

Ben was surprised that Madec apparently didn't hear the first muffled but loud explosion as the gas went up, the tent seeming to bulge with it.

The tent, made of fire-retardant fabric, burned slowly but with a great deal of smoke. Ben stood behind the Jeep, the slingshot in his hand, watching both the burning tent and Madec.

The man would *not* look around. A pillar of smoke went up on a long angle away from the butte and flames licked along the edges of the fabric but still Madec hung on the wall hammering.

And then the Coleman exploded, pieces of it tearing out across the sand.

Madec's head swung around.

For a moment he just hung there staring and then he came clambering down the rock wall and started running as soon as he hit the ground. He ran for about ten feet, then suddenly stopped, whirled back to the wall, grabbed the rifle and set out again.

Now, Ben thought as he put a buckshot into the leather holder, he's coming to me. The way I want him to.

14

BEN WATCHED MADEC carefully as he approached the stone slab, but the man did not take his eyes off the burning tent as he went past the place where Ben had been buried and came on, running, the gun balanced in his right hand.

Ben heard the tent collapse with a whoosh and the snapping noise of guy ropes burning through, but he did not take his eyes off Madec.

The man was in a fury, his eyes open and staring, his teeth gritted together.

When the tent finally went wearily down, Madec slowed and then, as though exhausted, began to walk, coming on pace by pace, the rifle hanging in his hand.

Ben knew that it had to be now.

He could feel the butt of his thumb through the dirty hairs of his beard as he drew his hand back.

The brace of the slingshot was a steady, unwavering, strong pressure against the inner side of his left arm.

Ahead, framing Madec as he came on, now a

little crouched as though stalking something, the yoke of the slingshot was firm.

Ben tried to make the release an instantaneous thing, no muscle of his hand or fingers moving before or after any other muscle.

Oddly, he did not know when the shot left, did not even hear the snap of the rubbers or the slap of the leather holder when it struck the Jeep fender.

He saw nothing through the yoke but Madec's right hand; in fact, he saw clearly only the row of knuckles where the fingers joined the hand. A row of little round hills, growing smaller, not quite as pink as the flat back of the hand or the rounded surface of the fingers.

The skin of the second knuckle peeled back and became stark white for a second and then red.

The rifle dropped straight down, bounced off Madec's right foot and rolled into the sand.

For a moment, as Ben loaded again, he lost sight of Madec, but when he looked again the man was doing a strange, awkward little dance out there in the sand. He was clinging to his right hand with his left and was hopping up and down, first on one foot and then the other. As he hopped he spun slowly around.

Suddenly the dance stopped and Madec was looking at him, his face wild with pain and fury.

The dance had moved him perhaps five feet from the rifle, and now he lunged toward it, his left arm reaching out for it, pulling the short-sleeved jacket tight around the muscles of his upper arm.

The double-O buckshot didn't make that little hard whistling sound stones made but went silently.

Madec howled as he jerked his arm back and fell to his hands and knees.

He was crawling toward the gun as Ben loaded again.

The lead buckshot hit him where the kneecap lay in its cup. It ripped through the cloth and across his knee, opening the flesh.

The man kept moving and Ben hit him again, the shot rattling across the knuckles of his extended left hand.

As Madec's right hand, the fingers red with blood, reached out and touched the stock of the rifle, the buckshot struck his right wrist, embedding itself in the tendons.

Madec, now flat on the desert, slowly pulled his hand back and under his chest as though to protect it.

With the slingshot loaded again, Ben stood up and, never taking his eyes off Madec, felt around on the tailgate until he found the leather pouch. Emptying some of the shot into his mouth, he put the pouch down again.

Madec, lying within reach of the rifle, turned his head in the sand and looked at him, the pale eyes cold, the skin of his freshly shaved face cold.

Ben drew the leather holder back to his chin and aimed directly at the uppermost eye. "Don't move again," he said, his words a little slurred by the shot in his mouth.

Ben circled carefully around him, aiming at him all the time, until he could reach the rifle.

He scraped it away from Madec with his foot until he could safely pick it up.

Holding the gun aimed point-blank at Madec, Ben unsnapped the leather sling and, flipping it over his shoulder, took the gun in both hands and walked around until he was behind Madec.

He looped the sling around Madec's ankles, drew it tight and knotted it.

As he backed away, Madec started to roll over. Ben spat the buckshot out into his hand and said, "I told you not to move. So don't move."

At the Jeep he got one of the canvas belts he used to lash the water cans in their racks and went back to Madec.

With the rifle muzzle pressed against the back of Madec's neck, Ben reached under him, got the bloody hands out and tied them behind him.

Not satisfied with the sling and belt, Ben went over to the butte. It was a simple matter to pull down the rope Madec had looped over the tent pegs. Carrying the rope and tool bag, Ben returned and tied Madec's wrists and ankles with the rope.

Rolling Madec over on his back, Ben searched the big flap pockets of the fancy bush jacket, finding keys to the suitcase and duffel and Jeep in one pocket, the rotor and Hornet bolt in another.

Ben put the rotor back in first and then un-locked the duffel bag and emptied it out on the sand. The old man's stained felt hat fell out first.

It hurt getting his feet into his boots but once they were on, his feet only ached a little.

Dressed, Ben tossed the slingshot into the front of the Jeep and went back to Madec, who was now sitting up in the sand. Getting him under the arms, he dragged him over to the Jeep, lifted him up and strapped him in with the seat belt.

During all this Madec only stared at him. It was not a look of anger; or of defeat, or of fear, it was a steady, cold, intelligent probing.

Ben had been right. The Jeep did not start at once, and he had to crank it three or four times before the engine caught and ran.

He wheeled the Jeep to the east and headed back toward the little range of mountains.

For the first time Madec spoke. "This isn't the way."

"It's the way," Ben said.

"Where are you going?"

"To get the old man."

"Oh," Madec said. "Yes."

Ben drove the Jeep up to the same place he had parked it before.

He took the rotor out and then took the bolt out of the .358, putting them in his pocket with the Hornet bolt.

Then he got the old tarpaulin from the floor of the Jeep and went up across the shale to the cliff.

The old man was not there, and it took Ben a little while to find where Madec had stuffed the naked body under an overhang of rock. Nobody, not even Les Stanton, could have seen him from the air—or on foot, unless he was looking for the body.

The vultures had not touched him yet but he was stiff in death, hard to wrap and harder to carry. There was a nauseating, sweetish smell coming from him as Ben carried him down and laid him in the back of the Jeep, lashing him in, for the tailgate couldn't be closed.

As Ben started the engine Madec said, "Aren't you going to help me?"

"Help you do what?" Ben asked, his hand on the gear shift lever.

"You've broken my hand. You've broken my wrist. You've broken my leg, and I'm bleeding profusely. Aren't you going to help me?"

Ben tried to hold back his anger as he put his hand on Madec's back and, restraining his desire to shove the man brutally forward, just pushed him enough to see his hands.

His right hand was a real mess; covered with sand and blood, the bone of his knuckle sticking out strangely clean and white. His left arm looked only bruised, a big, swollen purple place where the buckshot had torn through the muscle. It wasn't bleeding badly.

Pushing Madec back against the seat, Ben reached down and, taking the cloth beside the little hole the shot had made, tore open the khaki trousers. Madec's knee was in bad shape, bloody and torn.

Ben put the Jeep into gear and started very slowly down the slope. "There's nothing I can do for you," he said. "And you're not bleeding enough to make any difference."

On the floor of the desert, Ben turned west and worked up through the gears until the Jeep was going well in third, averaging about ten miles an hour.

When he reached the distant mountains, Ben knew, it would be slower going, all four-wheel drive, scrambling up and through a long, winding canyon. It was going to be late at night before they got home.

After a while Madec said, "I'm not in a very good position to make a deal with you, Ben, but let's talk."

"Go ahead."

"Have you thought this thing out?"

"I've thought some about it."

"I mean, all the way out. All the different ways."

"Go ahead," Ben told him.

"To you—because everything to you is simple and straightforward and honest—this entire little episode may seem just that, simple, straightforward, clean cut. No questions."

Madec paused for a long time. "I'm different," he said at last. "I guess you could say that I'm a liar, Ben. Yes, I guess some people could say a thing like that."

Ben saw Madec's head turn toward him and knew that Madec was looking at him. "I'm not a brand-new liar, either, Ben. I'm an old hand at it. I've had a lot of practice. As a matter of fact, some people consider me an expert at it. Now as we discuss this matter I want you to keep that in mind, Ben."

"It'll be easy."

"And I'm a survivor, Ben. That's something you don't know much about, but in the jungle I live in it takes a smart man to survive. You've got to be smart and shrewd and cold. And you've got to be a professional liar. It's a tough, mean world. . . . Ben, listen, I'm really in very great pain."

Ben turned for a second to look at him, wondering that he felt absolutely nothing for this man. No hatred, no desire for revenge, and no triumph, no sense of victory. Just—nothing. "So am I," he said. "And there's nothing we can do about it."

"You could loosen the rope on my hands, my hand is really in bad shape. Why do you need the rope anyway? I'm helpless. And I·might get gangrene this way."

"You might," Ben said.

"That's petty and mean," Madec said. "Real petty. I didn't think you were like that, Ben."

"I'm like that."

"I'll keep that in mind," Madec said and then was quiet for a long time.

"I suppose you're going straight to the sheriff," Madec said.

"That's right."

"And tell him exactly what happened?"

Ben nodded.

"Have you stopped to think that things have become a little more complicated since the other day, Ben?"

"Not to me, they haven't."

"Oh, yes, they have, Ben. You see, the other day I didn't have a broken hand and broken leg. I hadn't been viciously cut up. Not cleanly shot, mind you, as, in self-defense you might have shot me, but deliberately and viciously chopped up, tortured. Exactly the way you chopped up the old man, except you killed him. You see, Ben, things *have* changed."

"They sure have," Ben said.

"So I think we ought to talk some, Ben. Now, I don't know whether I told you this, but I'm a rich man. And I'm not stupid. I realize that by taking me in to the sheriff and telling your story you might get me into a little trouble. Note that I said you *might* get me into a little trouble. The fact is, that if you want to be stubborn about this, I believe I can get you into extremely serious trouble. In fact, I know I can, so don't sit there like God and think you've got this thing in the bag, my boy. You'll be a lot better off if you stop right here and we work this thing out."

"Would you like for me to take off my shoes and clothes and start out again with no water?" Ben asked.

Madec laughed. "It never happened, Ben," he

said pleasantly. "It's all a dream you had, a dream nobody will believe. Would you like to know what really happened, Ben?"

"Not your version of it," Ben told him. "So keep quiet now, will you? I'm busy."

Madec sat for a long time just staring out at the desert. At last he said, "Ben, listen to me, I'll give you ten thousand dollars if you'll stop right here and bury the old man and say nothing about it. I'm willing to bet ten thousand dollars that you'll keep your word. I'll write you a check for that amount right this minute. And I'll go with you to the bank and see that you get it—in cash."

"What'll you write it on?" Ben asked.

Madec snapped his head around and looked in the back of the Jeep. His voice was furious as he said, "Where's my suitcase?"

"Gone."

"Gone *where?*"

"It was in the tent. Where you left it."

Madec slumped in the seat. "Oh, you stupid yokel," he said. Then he straightened and said, "Forgive me, Ben. I'm really in great pain and don't mean what I say."

"I believe it," Ben said.

"Then believe this, too. I can go with you to any bank in the country and get ten thousand dollars—cash—in ten minutes."

"Oh, shut up," Ben said. "Just sit there and count your money."

15

For the last seven hours Ben had thought how happy he was going to be when he pulled that Jeep up in front of the sheriff's office. Only then would this thing finally end, only then would he be back among decent people.

The sheriff's office was in a small wooden building with some palo verde trees around it. As Ben swung the Jeep off the street, he saw three sheriff station wagons parked in the combination jail and garage behind the office.

He felt no happiness at all as he braked the Jeep to a stop. Instead, the ending of movement seemed to let a great weight of weariness fall on him. It took an effort to reach out and turn the ignition off. As he got out he staggered a little, holding the Jeep for balance. He ached all over and felt a little sick, cold spit running around his teeth.

"You're out of your mind!" Madec said in a choked, angry voice. "I have to go to a hospital, a doctor! Get *in!*"

Ignoring him, Ben walked stiffly across the dark parking lot.

The air-conditioning unit on the roof of the office was running rough, and he wondered why they didn't get it fixed—it seemed to be shaking the little building.

The sheriff's office was one large room with some closets and toilets on the right, a long wooden bench near the door, three desks and a businesslike radio built into one wall. To Ben the air felt very cold and dry and thick with stale cigarette smoke.

Ben had expected to find Sergeant Hamilton, the sheriff in charge, but the only person in the room was a young deputy named Strick who was sitting at one of the desks filling out some sort of form.

Strick—his full name was Eugene Strick but no one ever called him anything but Strick—had been in Ben's class in high school. A good-looking, rugged guy who, for as long as Ben could remember, had always wanted to be a sheriff. That alone had set him a little apart from the others in the class and no one, including Ben, really knew Strick very well.

Behind Strick on the wall was a big electric clock. They had made pretty good time; it was only a little past nine.

As Ben closed the door, Strick looked up and then stared at him. "Holy mack-e-rel, Ben, what happened?" he asked.

Ben had thought Hamilton would be there.

Ham was an old friend, a good hunting and fishing buddy and a warmer, more understanding man than Strick.

"What hit you, Ben?" Strick asked, getting up and coming over to look at him.

"Couple of mountains," Ben said. "Is Ham here?"

"No, he's gone home. Look, you go see the doctor and you can fill out any accidents reports when he gets through. You're in bad shape, Ben."

"I've got a dead man out in the Jeep," Ben told him. "And I've got the man who killed him."

"You got *what?*"

"Trouble," Ben said. "But he needs a doctor worse than I do so how about calling the D & T and see if anybody's there."

As Strick went back to his desk for his belt, he said, "The doc's there, I just sent him a head-on." He buckled on his belt. "You've got a dead man, you say. Who is he?"

"I don't know. An old man out on the desert. It was an accident."

Strick adjusted his belt, feeling for the butt of the pistol. "Let me just have a look, Ben, before we do any talking. With all these rules we've got to be real careful in things like this."

Strick put on his wide-brimmed hat, and Ben followed him out the door.

Outside in the dark they walked together over to the Jeep.

"Who's this?" Strick asked, pulling a flashlight out of a leather case on his belt and shining it in on Madec. Then he backed off. "Oh," Strick said. "It's you, Mr. Madec. How are you?"

"I've been shot. I need a doctor," Madec said.

"Yes, sir. You want to get out and come inside, sir?"

"How can I," Madec asked coldly. "My hands and feet are tied with a rope."

"What?" Strick said and then turned to Ben. "What's going on, Ben?"

"It's a long story, and he needs a doctor first."

Strick raised the flashlight and shone it in Ben's face. "Where's the dead man?"

Ben walked around to the back and unfolded the tarpaulin. Strick shone the light in on the old man's face. "Ugh," he said. "No idea who he is?"

"No. Just an old man. A prospector."

"You'd better come back inside," Strick said.

"Look, Strick, I'm hurt and so is Madec. I'll leave the old man here, and we'll go down to the Center."

Strick hesitated and then went back to Madec. "Where are you hurt, Mr. Madec?"

"Ben almost killed me," Madec said in a weak voice. "He broke my hand and broke my leg and just cut me to ribbons."

"What've you got him tied up for, Ben?" Strick asked, his voice unpleasant.

"Because he's dangerous."

"Who you kidding?" Strick said. "Untie him, and we'll take him down to the Center. I'll get a car."

As Strick went toward the garage, Ben leaned

in and pushed Madec forward so he could reach the rope.

"This is your last chance, Ben," Madec said in a low, quick voice. "Ten thousand dollars. Take it and your troubles are over. If you don't take it I'll see to it that you spend the next ten years in jail. I can do that to you, Ben, believe me, I can."

"I believe you," Ben said, untying his ankles.

"You won't take it."

"No."

"All right," Madec said as the station wagon moved toward them. "If you thought I was tough in the desert, you haven't seen anything yet."

Strick came over and gently helped Madec into the back seat of the wagon. "Just lie down there, sir. It's only a couple of blocks."

"Thank you, officer," Madec said.

As Strick got in he said, "You bring the Jeep, Ben. Take it around to the back where they can get that body out."

Ben followed the white wagon down to the brand-new Diagnostic & Treatment Center, which was the closest thing the town had to a real hospital.

As the station wagon drew up under the lights of the emergency entrance Ben drove on around to the back, parked and went over to the door. It was locked so he rang the bell and stood leaning against the wall until the door opened and a kid about nineteen named Souchek looked out. "You got the wrong door, Ben."

"I got a dead man in the Jeep."

"Wrong address, too," Souchek said. "We don't take 'em in, we carry 'em out."

He started to close the door, but Ben held it open. "Strick said bring him in."

"Who does Strick think he is! Yes, sir, Mr. Strick, anything you say, sir. Okay, I'll get something. What happened to him?"

"He got shot."

Souchek came back with a big canvas laundry basket on a dolly, and they lowered the old man, still wrapped in the tarpaulin, down into the basket and wheeled him into the building.

In the light Ben saw that the tarpaulin had fallen back and the old man's face, gray and shriveled-looking, was exposed, his mouth and eyes open.

Souchek flung a soiled sheet over the basket and said, "What happened to you?"

"I slid," Ben said. "Is Doc Myers here?"

"No, he's in Phoenix."

"Nobody here?"

"The Boy Genius is here."

That bothered Ben. All the way across the desert he had expected that Doc Myers would be here and would, in that way he had, take charge of everything. Doc Myers had seen it all, life, death, sickness, accidents; you couldn't shake him.

Everybody in town called this new doctor in the Center the Boy Genius. Ben had heard that he was the youngest man ever to graduate from the medical school at the University of California and had made the highest marks in the school's history, or something. And everybody in town wondered why such a genius had decided to come to work in this little dry and drying-up town on the edge of the desert. A doctor like him, a boy genius . . . There must be something wrong with him, the town decided, and there was a lot of talk, a lot of speculation and a lot of rumors.

His name was Saunders, and he was a thin, dark, intense man who had nothing to say to you if you weren't sick or hurt.

Ben had only met him once when his uncle had broken a finger in a Jeep transmission and didn't have any feeling about the doctor one way or the other. A little cold, maybe, a little haughty, but he seemed to know what he was doing.

He followed Souchek down the corridor to the emergency room and went in. Dr. Saunders, in a bloodstained green smock, and a nurse were in there and had Madec up on the table.

Under the bank of hard lights Madec looked pretty bad. His leg from the knee down was a mess of blood and dirt, and both his hands and arms were covered with blood.

Ben started over to the doctor but Strick saw him and put his hand on Ben's chest, pushing him back toward the door. "You stay outside," Strick told him. "You too, Souchek."

Outside the room, Ben pushed the laundry basket out of the way and sat down on a bench, stretching his legs out, his heels sliding along the floor. Souchek rolled the basket into a closet and came out with a big floor polisher. As he started unraveling the cord he said, "What'd you shoot him for, Ben?"

"I didn't," Ben said.

"Then who did?"

Ben motioned with his thumb toward the emergency room. "He did."

Souchek stared at him. "Shot *himself?*"

"Oh, him," Ben said. "No, I shot him."

"What for?"

"To keep him from shooting me."

"Oh, boy! What'd you guys do, find a gold mine or something, and then get into a fight about it?"

"Something like that," Ben said, letting his eyes fall shut. He had never felt so tired, so drained out in his life.

"You mind moving your feet so I can polish?" Souchek asked.

Without opening his eyes, Ben pulled his feet back, lifted them wearily and put them down on the bench.

The polisher made a hideous, screaming noise.

He must have fallen asleep, for it seemed that it was only a few seconds later that the door opened and Dr. Saunders wheeled Madec out on a rolling bed and took him down the corridor.

Then Strick came out and beckoned to him. "Your turn," he said and then followed Saunders and Madec into a room across the hall.

Ben had known the nurse, Emma Williams, all his life and as he came in said, "Hello, Emma."

She was putting a clean sheet on the high, narrow table and didn't say anything until she finished. Then she turned and looked at him. "That just goes to show you never can tell," she said and went on fussing around.

She must be as tired as I am, Ben thought, as he sat down on a little stool.

"Don't sit there," Emma said sternly.

Ben thought he wasn't going to make it up off the stool.

The doctor came in, glanced at him, and said, "Take off your clothes. Down to your shorts." Then he went over to a glass-doored cabinet and began taking things out of it.

"I haven't got on any shorts," Ben said.

The doctor glanced at him with a cold and disgusted look but didn't say anything. Emma, as though holding out a live snake, handed him a towel.

It was painful getting his shoes and socks off and his bare feet began to bleed on the floor as he got his pants off, wrapped the towel around himself and started to take off his shirt.

The cloth felt as though it had become his skin and, when he pulled at it, it felt as though he were ripping his skin off. It made him dizzy and he had to stop and hold on to the edge of the table to keep from falling down.

The doctor came over and with one quick,

painful yank stripped the shirt away. "Hmmm," the doctor said. "All right, get on the table. Face down."

The cool, clean sheet and hard table felt delicious. The doctor's hands touching him here and there hurt, but they were cool, gentle and strong. Ben heard him say crisply, "All right, nurse, before we start I want you to write this down."

"You better say it so those sheriffs can understand or you'll have to do it all over again," Emma said disagreeably.

"I know that," the doctor said, and Ben could feel the ice in it. "General abrasions across back, shoulders, buttocks and legs. Minor lacerations in same areas. The same condition on knees, hands, arms, and tops of feet and ..."

"Not so fast!" Emma said. ". . . arms and tops of what?"

"Feet," the doctor said, and began to talk more slowly. "Both feet cut, abraded and bruised, swollen but not infected. Two-inch-long, clean cut on left cheek just below the eye. Entire body sunburned but with negligible blistering." Then he flicked Ben on the shoulder with his fingertips and said, "Turn over."

Lying on his back, Ben looked at the doctor as he went on examining him and reciting to Emma what was wrong with him.

The doctor was so cold, so remote that it made Ben feel uncomfortable, as though, to the doctor, he wasn't even human.

Then he suddenly seemed interested as he picked up Ben's arm and looked at where Madec had shot him. "Hello, what's this?" he said, and turned the arm over. He clamped down with his fingers. "Hurt?"

"Yes, it does," Ben said, "but not much."

The doctor flexed Ben's arm, moving and twisting it as he felt the bones and tendons with his fingers. At last he laid it down on the table and said, "Lucky." Then he said, "Nurse, gunshot wound, left arm, three inches below the elbow, clean entrance and exit wounds, minor damage, no bones involved."

As the doctor swabbed out the purplish holes and then put adhesive bandages over them, Emma finished what she was writing and said, "You have to put in the report what to do with him."

"Except for injuries noted, the patient is in apparently good health and can be released to the custody of the sheriff," the doctor said.

Ben looked up at him, wondering why he had to be so unfriendly about everything.

The doctor said, without any sympathy, "This is going to hurt."

It hurt a lot and as Ben watched him sewing up the cuts on his feet, he wondered if the doctor had to be so rough about it. He rammed that curved needle through Ben's flesh as though he were sewing up a ripped tarpaulin.

He finished putting the bandages on and went out, saying to Emma, "I'll be in the lab if anybody wants me. You'd better see to Mr. Madec."

As Emma started across the room Ben said, "Is that all?"

"All of what?" she said and left.

Ben was half-dressed, standing on his bandaged feet, when Strick came in. He looked sore about something as he leaned against the wall waiting for Ben to finish.

Ben couldn't get his boots on over the bandages so picked them up. He felt sick and weak and very tired.

"You know what I'm going to do, Strick?" he said. "I'm going home and go to bed and sleep for a week. One week."

"Let's go down to the office first. I've got to get some sort of statement from you about all this."

"Tomorrow," Ben said. "I'm really bushed, Strick."

"Tonight would be better," Strick said. "While it's fresh in your mind."

Ben smiled, and his lips felt as though they hadn't smiled for years. They were stiff and they hurt. "That's going to be fresh in my mind for the next fifty years."

But Strick beckoned him to come and in the corridor headed him toward the front door. "What about my Jeep?" Ben asked.

"It's been impounded as evidence."

In the station wagon Ben said, "How's Madec?"

"What do you care?" Strick asked unpleasantly.

"What are you so sore about, Strick?" Ben asked.

Strick glanced at him as he turned in at the sheriff's office. "I try not to let it get to me, but sometimes the things people do to each other make me mad," he said.

In the office Strick went around behind his desk and sat down, motioning to Ben to sit in the chair in front of him. Picking up a piece of cardboard, Strick began to read from it rapidly and tonelessly. It was something about Ben's rights, that he could have an attorney, that he did not have to confess to anything if he didn't want to.

Strick put the cardboard down and said, "Do you understand what I just read to you?"

"That's why I'm here," Ben said. "There was an accident, and I'm reporting it. I don't need a lot of stuff about my rights, and I don't need any lawyers."

"Hold it! Hold it!" Strick cautioned him. "If you want to talk to me here's a waiver for you to sign. Just sign it right there." He pushed a blank form across the desk.

"What for?"

"It just says you heard me read to you about your rights, and you understand what I read and are waiving 'em."

Ben signed it, and Strick took it back and put it in his drawer. Then he sat back in the chair, his arms over his head and said, quietly, "Why did you shoot him so many times, Ben?"

Ben could see Madec again, coming toward him, the big gun swinging in his hand. Then he saw Madec down on the sand, still reaching for that gun. "To keep him from shooting me," Ben said.

"Then how can that be an accident?"

For a moment Ben was confused. "Wait a minute, Strick. Who are you talking about?"

"The old man," Strick said.

"I'm talking about Madec."

Without any change in his voice or position, Strick said, "All I'm trying to do is find out what happened, Ben. What was the beef between you and that old man?"

Half of Ben's face was numb from the novocaine. It felt as though spit were running out of the left side of his mouth, but he couldn't stop it. Suddenly it was hard for him to think about all this; it seemed so long ago. "Beef?" he asked. "I didn't even know that old man."

"All right, then let's go back to Mr. Madec. How many times did you have to shoot him, Ben?"

Ben tried to remember. "I don't know, Strick. Once to make him drop the gun, and a couple more times when he kept going for it. Three? Four?"

"You shot him more than once, though, is that right?"

"Yeah. Look, Strick, I'm really wiped out. Let's wait until tomorrow and then go through the whole thing."

"Be a lot easier to get it over with now."

"I can't even think straight now," Ben said. "Tomorrow." He pushed himself up out of the chair. "Give me a call when you're ready, and we'll go through the whole thing."

As Ben started toward the door Strick said quietly, "Where're you going, Ben?"

"Home."

"I can't let you do that, fella," Strick said.

Ben turned to look at him.

Strick was writing something and said, without looking up at him, "I'm charging you with felony-aggravated assault, Ben."

"Okay," Ben said and started toward the door again, wondering what walking around in the bandages was doing to them. Then he stopped and looked back at Strick. "With *what?* What does that mean?"

"It means you're not going home," Strick said, his voice different now; tough. "It means you're going to jail."

16

THE JAIL WAS a one-room cell with concrete walls, a barred steel door, two bunks, a washbasin and a toilet.

Ben was so tired that all he could do was stagger over to the empty bunk, sit down on it and begin to laugh. The only thing he could think about was that his old classmate, Strick, had put him in jail. Somehow it seemed funny.

What was it Strick had said he'd done? Felony? And assaulting something. And aggravation.

It was aggravation, all right, he thought.

He knew that he should be outraged by the injustice of all this. He should be angry and doing something about it, but, as he let sleep come rolling in, he felt as he had in the desert; that it was not real, was not happening.

Tomorrow everything will get straightened out, he thought. Tomorrow.

When he woke up it was broad daylight. The door of the cell was open, and a deputy Ben didn't know was standing out in the corridor.

A kid in Ben's Boy Scout troop named Don Smith came in with a tray of food and when he saw Ben almost dropped it. Not saying a word, he just stared at Ben as he put the tray down on the bunks and backed out of the cell.

"Has anybody called my uncle?" Ben asked the deputy.

"I'll check the log," the deputy said and shut the door.

The food was good. When he finished Ben went to the door and tried to see out but could see nothing except the wall across a narrow corridor.

It was a long time before Ben heard someone coming down the corridor.

His uncle, looking worried and sad, peered in through the bars. "Ben," he said in a sort of wailing voice, "what have you done?"

"Nothing," Ben told him. "See if you can get hold of Ham. Not Strick. Ham."

"He's here," his uncle said. "He'll be ready for you in a minute. But listen, Ben, don't say anything, hear? I'm going to get you a lawyer; I called Joe McCloskey as soon as I heard, but he can't get here until tomorrow. So just don't say anything until he gets here."

"I've got nothing to hide," Ben said.

"Just don't say anything. How bad are you hurt, Ben?"

"I'm okay. I just want out of here, Unc. Go tell Ham I want out."

"All right. But remember, Ben, don't say anything."

Ben watched his uncle's face disappear. He was a good man, Ben thought, a good, honest, sad man who still seemed to hope that his wife who had hated the desert and had walked out on him twenty years before, was going to come back—about any minute now.

Ben got madder and madder as time passed, and no one else came to the door. Around ten o'clock the Boy Scout and the deputy came back to take the tray. As soon as the door opened Ben said, "Listen, Deputy, does Ham know I'm in here?"

The deputy just looked at him and said, "Get the tray, Don."

"I asked you! Does Ham know I'm in here?"

"He knows," the deputy said, letting Don out and closing the door.

It was an hour later before Sergeant Hamilton came and unlocked the door. "I'm sorry to see you in all this trouble, Ben. Come on in the office."

"There wouldn't be any trouble if you'd been here last night, Ham," Ben said. "Things are just all fouled up."

"Yeah," Ham said, closing the cell door. "How you feeling, Ben?"

"Fine."

"Can you walk okay?"

"Sure. Look, Ham, what's Madec saying? What kind of story is he telling?"

"We'll go into it," Ham said as they walked slowly across the hot pavement.

"Whatever it is, it's a lie, Ham."

There was a crowd in the office. His uncle, Les Stanton, the game warden, Mr. Hondurak, the justice of the peace, Strick, Denny O'Neil, the chopper pilot, and two men in suits Ben had never seen before. He looked around for Madec, but he wasn't there.

"Sit down, Ben," Ham said.

There was silence in the room for a moment as everybody stared at him and then the justice of the peace, Mr. Hondurak, said, "All right, Ben. First, these are Mr. Madec's attorneys. Mister . . ."

The older of the two men in suits pointed with his thumb at the younger one and said, "Alberts, and I'm Mr. Barowitz."

Ben nodded to them but neither of them even glanced at him. He studied them a moment as they sat, looking pale and bloated among all these leather-skinned, desert-dry men.

"Now, Ben," Hondurak said, "Officer Strick tells me you've been informed of your rights, and here's the waiver you signed."

Ben nodded.

"If you want to, I'd like to hear your version of this thing," Hondurak said.

As Ben started to speak he noticed Sonja O'Neil for the first time. She was sitting at Strick's desk, her hands poised over a stenotype machine.

Sonja and that machine made him nervous, but he told his story slowly, trying to remember each detail, trying to keep everything in sequence. No one said anything, but just sat looking at him, as Sonja kept making soft clicking noises with the machine, the paper folding itself up neatly as it came out.

When he got to the point where they had found the old man on the ridge the sheriff spoke for the first time. "Was he dead?"

"Yes, sir."

"Shot?"

"Yes, sir."

"How many times?"

"Once."

"You're sure of that?"

"Yes, sir."

"Where?"

"In the chest."

Ben went on with it, telling them only what had happened after that, leaving out what he had thought and felt; leaving out both his fear of Madec and his anger.

The sheriff was the only one who asked any questions. "What did you shoot Mr. Madec with?"

"The slingshot, sir."

"The one you found in the old man's camp?"

"Yes, sir."

"Where is that slingshot, Ben?"

"In the Jeep."

Ben saw Ham glance over at Strick, who shook his head.

"Isn't it in the Jeep?" Ben asked.

"There's no slingshot in the Jeep."

"Then it must have fallen out when we took the old man out," Ben said.

"It didn't," Strick said.

"It's either out on the ground in the parking lot or back behind the Diagnostic Center," Ben said. "Because it was in the Jeep when I got here. I saw it."

"There's no slingshot," Strick said. "Anywhere."

"Go ahead, Ben," Hamilton said.

"It's around somewhere. A hunting slingshot with a brace that comes down on your arm."

"I mean, what happened then?" the sheriff said.

"That's about all," Ben said. "I got the gun away from him and tied him up. Then I went back and got the old man and brought him in."

The sheriff looked over at the justice of the peace, who said, "Les, how about you and Strick going out there in the chopper, and check some of these details, will you? See if you can find where the old man was shot. Pick up any slugs you find. Check on his camp. You might look that butte over a little, too, just in case. And if you can find where Ben shot Madec, pick up any slugs there, too."

"Let me go along," Ben said. "I can show you."

"That's all right, Ben," Ham said. "You just stay here."

Ben looked around at them, and suddenly he felt as though the hot, stale room was ice cold.

None of them would look at him. It was frightening.

He turned to Hondurak. "What did Madec tell you? What's his story?"

"Well, that isn't exactly relevant, Ben," Hondurak said.

"It is to me," Ben told him. "If you believe what he says, I can be in trouble."

"It isn't a question of whether I believe what he says, or what you say. This is just a preliminary investigation into the death of one man and an assault on another. I'm just trying to get all the details so I can decide whether there's a basis for a felony-aggravated assault charge and perhaps a suspicion of murder charge."

"Nobody got murdered," Ben told him. "It was an accident."

For the first time one of the lawyers, Barowitz, spoke. "Shooting a man three times is an accident?" he asked in a dry, low voice.

"Shooting a man after he's dead isn't a murder," Ben said.

The lawyer just shrugged and smiled at Hondurak.

"Ben, listen," his uncle said, "don't say any more. I'll get you a lawyer."

"I don't need a lawyer," Ben said. "I told you how this thing happened, and you can go out in the desert and see where it happened. If Madec told you something else, he's a liar."

"All right, all right, calm down," Hondurak

said. "Okay, lock him up, Strick, and then you guys get going."

"Why do I have to stay in jail?" Ben asked, trying to keep his voice down. "Where's Madec? He's not in jail!"

Hondurak looked at him coldly and said, "He's just as much in jail as you are, only he's been pretty badly shot up and is in the hospital."

"I should've . . ." Ben started to blurt out that he should have killed him, but stopped.

"Should have—what?" Barowitz asked.

"Never gone out in the desert with a liar like that," Ben said, getting up out of the chair as Strick beckoned to him.

When he was back in the cell his uncle came to the door and leaned on it, his fingers around the iron bars. "Ben," he said, "you know you can talk to me. Tell me the truth now. It's the only way."

"I told it," Ben said.

His uncle shook his head slowly from side to side. "It sure didn't sound like it in there, Ben. It sounded kind of fantastic. Kind of made up, Ben."

"That's the way it was when it was happening, too." Ben went over to the door. "What did Madec tell them?"

"Well, the sheriff and Hondurak won't talk to me about it, Ben. I guess they can't, legally. But I talked some to Emma Williams at the Center, and she says that she heard everything Mr. Madec told them. . . . It sure sounds bad, Ben. His story is a lot different from yours. And his makes a lot more sense."

"Like how?"

"Mr. Madec says you got sore at the old man. Claimed he'd run off the bighorn you were after. And that you scuffled around some and the old man hit you in the face with his metal locator and knocked you over a little cliff. That's how you got all those cuts and bruises."

"Oh, boy," Ben said.

"Then Mr. Madec says that after you and he got back to the Jeep, you took your Hornet and went off alone, saying you were going to hunt up the sheep again. And he says he felt pretty sore when he heard a couple of shots because it was supposed to be him out there hunting bighorn, not you. So he went up on the ridge. And you'd shot the old man."

Ben leaned against the wall. "He makes it sound so simple," he said.

"Yes, he does, Ben. Then Mr. Madec says you tried to make him believe it was an accident, shooting that old man, but you had shot him twice and when he argued with you about it, you got sore."

Ben suddenly felt better. "So how does he explain that the man was shot three times, not just twice? And once with a gun a lot bigger than a Hornet. How does he explain that?"

"That's what makes it so bad, Ben," his uncle said, in that slow, sad way of his. "Real bad, be-

cause Mr. Madec says you took his gun away
from him and shot the old man again, with his
gun, claiming that now you could prove it was
Mr. Madec and not you who had killed the old
man."

Ben couldn't stop the feeling that Madec was
outwitting him, outthinking him again. "It's all
a lie," he said helplessly.

His uncle just stared at him, looking as though
he was about to cry. "I sure hope so, Ben. Because then Mr. Madec says that when he realized
what you were trying to do to him he tried to get
away, get back to the Jeep. And that's when you
shot him and kept on shooting him until he
stopped running."

"If I did all that," Ben said, trying to imagine
the scene Madec had created for Hondurak and
Strick and Ham. "If I did all that, and that's the
way it really happened, then why was I such a
fool? Why did I go to all the trouble to bring him
in to the sheriff? If I'd already murdered that old
man, what difference would it have made to me
to murder Madec too? You see, Unc, he doesn't
make sense. He's lying."

"It sure doesn't sound like it," his uncle said.
"Mr. Madec says that you *had* to bring him in;
that you wanted to kill him but were afraid to."

"Afraid of *what?*" Ben demanded. "Wouldn't I
be more afraid of what he'd say alive?"

"You were afraid of Les and Denny," his uncle
said. "Because, just after you'd shot the old man,
they went over you in the chopper and you

couldn't be sure they hadn't seen what you'd done, with the old man right there dead on the ground. So you had to blame it on Mr. Madec. You couldn't kill him because you had to bring him in to make your story look good."

"To make his look good." Ben turned away from the door. "I should've done it."

"Now, now, Ben," his uncle said. "That's what's caused all the trouble. You know you've got a real hot temper."

"Not that hot." Ben turned back. "Unc, it's all a lie! All of it. They can't believe that!"

"They do. They can't say right out they do, but they do. The best thing for you to do is just hush now and wait for Joe McCloskey. Then, Ben—tell him the truth."

Ben went over to the bunk and sat down. After a moment he raised his head. "Les and Denny came down in the chopper and talked to Madec. How does he explain that?"

"I just told you. You had just shot the old man when they got there, but Madec didn't know that. He thought you were shooting bighorn, and he griped to them about it. They went off to look for you."

"In the wrong direction. You know something, Unc," Ben said quietly, "I didn't tell Hondurak and Ham all of it. I left out a lot. About how Madec tried to pretend he hadn't shot that man. About his trying to bribe me. He offered me ten thousand dollars. What about all that?"

"*Ten thousand dollars!*" His uncle shook his

head. "It sounds like all the rest of it, Ben. Kind of fantastic. If I were you, I wouldn't say anything about that. About anything. Wait till Joe gets here and talk to him. He can tell you what to do."

Ben looked at this man he had lived with for most of his life. "I don't think you believe me."

His uncle lowered his eyes. "I don't think you'd deliberately kill anybody. For no reason. But if a man knocked you down with a locator . . . well you've got an awful hot temper."

Ben lowered his head. "Okay, Unc," he said.

"I'll see you later, Ben."

"Yeah," Ben said.

Around one o'clock the deputy and the Boy Scout turned up again. As the boy came in with the food Ben said, "Don, do me a favor, will you? Go down to the Diagnostic Center and ask that kid down there—I think his name's Souchek—to look in . . ."

"Now, wait just a minute, fella," the deputy said at the door. "Nothing like that, fella."

Ben turned on him. "Who's side are you on?"

"I'm not on anybody's side so just you cool it."

"Okay," Ben said, "so *you* go ask that guy who cleans up down there to look in the trash and see if there's a slingshot in it."

"A slingshot!" the deputy said, disgusted. "You're asking somebody to root around in the trash for a slingshot?"

Ben walked to the door. The deputy must have

thought he was trying to escape; he stepped over to block the door and put his hand on his gun. Ben stopped in front of him and said, "A man claims I shot him with a rifle. I didn't. I shot him with a slingshot. If I can find it I can prove it. So I'll appreciate it if you will help me find it."

"If I get time," the deputy said, letting Don out and closing the door.

The long day dragged on and it was well after dark before the deputy and Don Smith came in with the evening meal.

Ben went to the door. "How about that sling-shot?"

"I haven't had time."

"It would be good if somebody looked before the trash gets picked up," Ben said.

"Maybe, after I get off duty," the deputy said, letting Don out and locking the door again.

Ben sat down and put the tray on his knees. He wasn't hungry, but eating was something to do.

He had seen that slingshot between the Jeep's front seats. . . .

He unfolded the paper napkin. Written on the inside of it, in pencil, was:

Can't find the slingshot. Looked every place. Don

What had Madec done with it? He'd only had a few seconds to hide it.

Ben was still eating, not enjoying the food,

when Strick came and opened the door.

"I've got to find that slingshot, Strick."

Strick stood at the door waiting, his hand on the butt of his pistol. "You walk in front of me," he said menacingly.

"I'm not some sort of thug," Ben said.

"Just walk in front of me."

In the office they were all there again, Hondurak, Sergeant Hamilton, his uncle, Sonja with her machine, Les Stanton and Denny O'Neil, and the two lawyers. Madec was not there.

"Where's Madec?" Ben demanded.

Nobody answered him, and Strick said, "Sit down."

"Okay, Strick," Hondurak said, "what'd you find out there?"

"All the evidence checks with Mr. Madec's story," Strick said, going over to Hondurak and handing him two smashed but recognizable full-patch bullets. "We'll send these in to ballistics but I'm pretty sure they're slugs from a Hornet. I found them on the ridge where Mr. Madec says Ben killed the old man. There're plenty of traces, blood all over, looked like somebody had a fight up there."

"No other slugs?" Hondurak asked. "Ben claims the man was killed with the .358."

"I already told you," Ben said. "Madec found that one and put it in his pocket."

Strick looked over at him and said, "That's what you did tell us, isn't it?" Then he held out his hand with the .358 slug lying in it. "I found this right near the other two. It's a .358."

Ben hardly heard Hondurak say, "Was this open ground, Strick? I mean, could Les and Denny have seen the body from the chopper?"

"I'm coming to that," Strick said. "There is distinct evidence that the body of that old man had been picked up and shoved in under a little overhang of rock so it couldn't be seen—not from a chopper."

"That's where Madec put him," Ben said.

They all seemed to ignore him. It was as though he hadn't said anything.

"Next," Strick said, "we found the old man's camp. It was a wreck. Somebody had just kicked it all to pieces. His blanket all ripped up, his clothes ripped up. Water can busted in, oven busted. Just a mess. But"—he paused and looked over at Ben—"there was no little tin box. No little tin box anywhere."

Ben looked over at Hondurak. "Am I allowed to ask anything?"

"Sure, go ahead."

Ben turned to Strick. "You say there was a blanket at the camp. Any shoes?"

"An old pair of boots, real beat-up, though."

"If they'd been there when I was there, why didn't I take them?" Ben asked. "I was naked. I could've used the blanket. I could have used any kind of boots."

The lawyer, Barowitz, said pleasantly, "Doesn't it seem to you, your honor, that this young man is contradicting himself? If, as he claims, *if* he was as naked and shoeless as he claims he certainly would have taken those boots, no matter in what condition. And, as he just said, he could have used pieces of the blanket. The fact that he left all that stuff there seems to argue that he was not, shall we say, as naked as he claims he was."

Ben felt as though he were talking inside a box or something. That nothing he said was being heard, nothing was being understood. "That's what I just *said!*" Ben yelled at them. "Madec went back later and put all that stuff there. When I . . ."

"For heaven's sakes, man, *why?*" Barowitz asked. "For what purpose would Mr. Madec maneuver all that junk around?"

"When I went to that camp there was nothing there," Ben said stubbornly.

"Including, I suppose, that mysterious little box containing that mysterious, vanishing slingshot," Barowitz said.

"Okay, okay," Hondurak said. "Let's don't get into any arguments, fellas. This is just an investigation. . . . What about the butte, Strick?"

"I'm not arguing!" Ben said. "I'm just . . ."

"We'll come back to that in a minute, Ben," Hondurak said. "All I want is to get the bare bones laid out, and then we can see what we've got. So, about the butte, Strick?"

"Nobody climbed that butte," Strick said in that loud, positive voice Ben remembered from high school. "Somebody tried, driving tent pegs in the wall and cutting some footholds, but nobody climbed it."

"I climbed it," Ben said.

Strick looked over at him. "Not up those tent pegs you didn't, they didn't go high enough."

"I climbed the other side."

Strick smiled at him. "First you say you were running around out there naked, and now you say you climbed that butte, bare-handed and buck naked. Well, I tell you nobody without mountain-climbing gear could get up there. Isn't that right, Les?"

"I couldn't," Les Stanton said.

"I did," Ben said.

"All right, all right," Hondurak said. "Now, Ben says he walked from the mountains over to the butte. Did you see any tracks of that, Strick?"

"Les says he thinks there're some tracks, but they sure don't look like tracks to me."

"Les?" Hondurak asked.

"There are tracks," Les said. "I can't swear to what made 'em, they're very indistinct. But if Ben was wearing sotol sandals the way he says, he might have made tracks like those."

"Les is an expert," Strick said, "but those things didn't look like man tracks to me, sandals or no sandals."

Ben watched Les, but he only shrugged his shoulders.

"Now, at the campsite," Hondurak said.

"They'd been there two or three days," Strick

said, "so it was pretty messed up, you couldn't tell nothing from nothing."

"No slugs from the Hornet?"

"Nobody shot the Hornet," Ben said.

"If there're any there it'll take awhile to find 'em," Strick said. "We can go back when we've got more time."

"Well," Hondurak said, "it looks to me like we've got evidence that the old man was shot twice by a Hornet rifle up on the ridge and that Mr. Madec was shot by a Hornet rifle down on the desert." He looked over at the two lawyers sitting together on the bench. "So it looks to me like we're going to have to prefer some charges here. For the old man, suspicion of murder and, for Mr. Madec, felony-aggravated assault."

Ben jumped up. "Wait a *minute!* You're not even listening. You're not even asking anybody anything. You . . ."

"Ben! Ben! Ben!" his uncle said to him. "Remember what I told you. Now hush up, Ben."

Ben ignored him and walked over to where Les Stanton was sitting in a chair, his long legs stretched out in front of him. He drew them in as Ben came closer.

"Les, did you go up on that butte?"

"Yeah, we landed up on top of it."

"Did you see that tunnel, about fifty feet down from the top, an old water tunnel with a catch basin in it?"

Les didn't answer for a long time and didn't look up at Ben as he finally said, "Don't you remember, Ben? The day you and I flew over that butte, and I showed you the catch basin in that tunnel?"

"Les," Ben said, "that's why I went there. That's why I had to get up there. For the water."

Mr. Barowitz smiled and slowly shook his head. "Now that explains a great many things," he said. "For example, it explains how you could describe that area very accurately—without ever having been in that tunnel!"

"I was in it," Ben said.

Les kept looking down at the floor. "You couldn't have reached that water using those tent pegs, Ben. You couldn't have done it."

"I didn't. I came the other way."

Les still didn't look up. "Ben, I'm not calling you a liar, but a man couldn't get into that tunnel from the other side."

There was no use trying to convince them, Ben decided. He had to prove it to them. "Did you go down into the tunnel?" he asked.

"I roped down to it."

For years Ben had thought of Les as one of the best and most honest of men, and the most desert-smart man he'd ever known. People liked to say that Les could track a bat.

"While I was in that tunnel," Ben said, making his voice stay level and quiet, "I shot eleven birds with that slingshot. And I ate 'em. And left the bones. Did you see any bones, Les?"

Les didn't say anything, just sat there frowning.

Ben couldn't believe it. Les wouldn't miss anything as obvious as those bones. "Gambel's quail," Ben said.

At last Les looked up. "There might have been bones, I just didn't see any, Ben. It was getting pretty dark in there."

Ben stared at him. "Then a whiptail lizard? I shot and ate one of those, too. Except the skin."

"I didn't see it, Ben," Les said.

"Les, go back up there, will you? First thing in the morning. . . ."

Barowitz said calmly, "Your honor, I suggest that since this is not a trial but simply a hearing, we can avoid confusion by not dealing with minor details."

Ben whirled on him. "They are not *minor* details! If there are bones up in that tunnel it proves I was there and not where Madec says I was." He turned back to Les. "We've got to get 'em, Les, before something else does. . . ."

"Ben," Hondurak said firmly. "I'll handle this, if you please."

"But don't you see, sir? If there are bones . . ."

"May I interject something here?" Barowitz said. "Don't birds sometimes die a natural death, your honor?"

As Ben started to yell at him, the sheriff held up his hand, but kept on reading from a notebook in his lap. "Now here's what Mr. Madec said. That during the first couple of days you two were out in the desert you, Ben, were fooling around that butte. He says he doesn't know whether you climbed it or not because he was off hunting bighorn, but you tried to climb it."

"*Fooling around!*" Ben shouted and then lowered his voice. "If I was just fooling around, Ham, would I have eaten raw birds? And a raw lizard?"

Barowitz said, looking at Hondurak, "Although I agree with your honor that these details should be left to the court I would like to suggest that the mere presence of some bird bones does not in any way identify the person who ate the meat from them. In fact, and I bow to you men's far wider experience in the desert, I think you will all agree that the mere presence of bones doesn't even establish how they got there, or how the bird died, or what happened to the carcass."

"Yeah," Hondurak said. "Sit down, Ben. You know I'm real sorry about this, but you can see how things look. And I'm just the justice of the peace, Ben, and this isn't a court, this isn't final. All I'm doing is establishing whether there's enough evidence to hold somebody. You see?"

"There's plenty," Ben said. "But not to hold me."

"Now sit down, Ben," Hondurak said sternly.

Ben sat down slowly, looking from man to man. The two lawyers were busy gathering up their briefcases and straightening their ties. Les just sat frowning down at the floor. Sergeant Hamilton had moved over and was talking quietly to Strick. Hondurak sat at the desk writing something.

No one was looking at him, not even Denny O'Neil, who was looking at his watch, or Sonja, who was gathering up the narrow folds of paper.

If these people who were once my friends will not believe me, will not even listen to me, Ben thought, what chance have I got when they take me out of this town and we go into a court at the county seat where nobody knows me?

Madec was so *good*. Everything was tied together, neatly and logically, with evidence to prove it.

And then Ben remembered. His voice sounded high and excited as he said, "Mr. Hondurak! Let me ask Les one more thing."

"Now, Ben . . ."

"Just one thing."

"Okay, make it short."

"Les," Ben said, "when you came down in the chopper where did Madec say I was?"

"In the mountains. He said you'd been shooting bighorn, and he was pretty sore about it."

"How far away from the chopper?"

Les looked over at Denny. "Seven, eight miles?"

"About seven," Denny said.

"So I couldn't have seen you?"

"What is the point of all this?" Barowitz asked.

"You wait," Ben snapped at him. "Les, could I have seen you?"

"Well, you could've seen the chopper."

"No, I mean *you*. What you had on, what you were wearing."

"Well, I don't know, Ben. No, I guess not. Not from seven miles."

Ben looked over at Barowitz. Now, for the first time, he felt good, felt as though he were physically breaking out of this trap Madec had made for him.

"All right!" Ben said triumphantly. "But if I *had* been on the butte I could have seen you?"

"Sure. We landed right at the base of it."

"All right! If I can tell you exactly what you had on then, I wasn't in the mountains, was I? I was on the butte."

Barowitz was standing up, as though ready to leave. "This is all very interesting," he said, "but I wonder if it takes much imagination to describe the uniform a game warden wears?"

Ben just stood grinning at Barowitz as Hondurak said, "That's a point."

"Is it?" Ben asked. "Because Les didn't have on his uniform. Did you, Les? You had on a purple shirt and yellow pants. And you had on white shoes. Didn't you, Les?"

Les looked embarrassed. "Well, I had to take Clayton's patrol at the last minute."

Ben turned to Hondurak. "You see, sir, Madec is lying. Everything he's said is a lie."

"*Mr. Hondurak!*" Barowitz said, hurrying over to him. "I have to object to this sort of language, sir. I really do."

"Now just calm down, Ben. . . . Les, what about it? Did you have on white shoes and a— purple shirt?"

Les laughed. "I go on patrol out of uniform one day in my life, and I wind up in the sheriff's office."

"I couldn't have been in the mountains where Madec claims I was," Ben said. "So if one of the things he said is wrong, why can't all the things be wrong?"

As Barowitz walked across the room to the gun case on the wall, Hondurak said, "Now, take it easy, Ben. . . ."

Barowitz turned with Ben's Hornet in his hands. He examined it a second and then said, "Quite a powerful telescopic sight on this rifle. I should think it would be quite easy to see what a man was wearing through a telescope like this."

"Not from seven *miles!*" Ben yelled.

Barowitz held the gun up and looked through the scope. "I'm sure I could," he said, putting the gun back.

The other lawyer spoke for the first time. "Or he could have been much closer but not on the butte. After all, he had left the camp some hours before. He could have been anywhere in the desert. Close enough to see what a man was wearing."

Barowitz came back and picked up his briefcase. "I think you've made a wise decision, your honor, to charge this man. So, good night, sir."

"Good night, good night," Hondurak said absentmindedly.

As the door closed Hondurak slowly looked over at Ben. "I'm really sorry about this, Ben, but you see how it is. I've got to bind you over for trial."

"No," Ben said. "I don't see. Madec shot the old man, and I shot Madec to keep him from shooting me. So I don't see why I'm the only one being accused around here."

"Okay, Strick," Hondurak said, "lock him up."

17

His uncle's voice sounded faint and far away, a voice talking nonsense in a dream. "It's all right, Ben. You'll have a lawyer. It's all right, boy."

Ben looked at Strick. "Now I guess you really want me to walk in front of you."

"Move," Strick said.

Ben was reaching for the doorknob when the door opened, and Dr. Saunders came in. He was wearing the green smock with his instruments sticking out of the pockets.

Ben turned back to Hondurak. "Maybe the doctor knows something."

The doctor looked at him as though he were some sort of bug and walked on by him, going toward Hondurak.

"Walk," Strick said.

But again the door was blocked by the two lawyers coming back in.

"Hold it, Strick," Hondurak said.

Ben stopped and turned around. The doctor was standing in front of Hondurak. He had his arms crossed and was looking down at Hondurak the same way he had looked at Ben. "I don't like being sent for," the doctor said.

Hondurak seemed surprised. "I'm sorry, I didn't mean it to sound that way, Doc. I just thought you could help us."

"Do what?'"

The two lawyers came up and stood behind the doctor.

Hondurak said, "These are Mr. Madec's lawyers. Mr. . . . ."

The doctor turned around and smiled. He held out his hand to Barowitz and they shook hands cordially.

"How are you, Doctor?" Barowitz asked.

"Did they fix you up in the motel all right?" the doctor asked.

"Perfect, thanks to you."

"It was nothing," the doctor said, smiling. "A pleasure." Then he turned to face Hondurak and Ben saw all the haughtiness, the coldness come back into his manner. "Now, what did you want with me?" he demanded.

Hondurak said to no one in particular, "We need a doctor's report on this matter." Then he looked up at Saunders. "I mean, anything you can give us as evidence."

"What's involved?" the doctor snapped.

He was so cold, Ben thought, so hostile as he stood staring steadily at Hondurak.

Hondurak seemed intimidated. "Well, it's a serious matter," he said apologetically. "There's suspicion of murder and aggravated assault."

The doctor half-turned and stared at Ben coldly for a long time. "Justified," he said.

Ben looked steadily back at him and said quietly, "I guess you want me to be scared of you, too, Doc. I'm not. I want . . ."

"Ben," the sheriff said, "I've had enough of that. I don't want any more interruptions from you."

Ben turned to look at him. "Ham, I'm accused of murder. Haven't I even got a right to try to defend myself?"

"You'll get your day in court," the sheriff said.

"If it's anything like this one I'll be in jail the rest of my life," Ben said.

"Ben," Hondurak said, "if you don't keep quiet I'll have you locked up, and I'll also charge you with contempt. Now *keep quiet*." He lowered his voice and said politely, "All right, Doctor. . . ."

The doctor turned to look at Ben. "This man has abrasions on his back, buttocks, arms, legs, feet and knees. These abrasions were made when there was nothing—no fabric or other material—between his skin and whatever was scraping against him. In other words, he was naked at the time. The lacerations of his feet and the cut on his cheek were apparently made by sharp stones. There were grains of sand in his hair, beard, ears and pubic area."

"Interesting," Barowitz said. "Tell me, Doctor,

could those injuries have been caused by being hit in the face with a heavy metal locator which knocked him off a cliff down on some rather sharp stones?"

"Possibly," the doctor said, and then added, "If he had been naked at the time he fell."

Barowitz smiled at him. "Now, Doctor wouldn't that be a little difficult to prove? Under oath?"

"I could have proved it last night when I cleaned the areas. I can't prove it now."

"I didn't think you could," Barowitz said.

The doctor shrugged and went on. "This man had also suffered from extreme dehydration and had been exposed for a considerable time to the sun, while naked."

"If you remember, sir," Barowitz said to Hondurak, "Mr. Madec complained in his statement that this man he had hired to take him hunting wasted a great deal of their time lying about, nude, taking sunbaths."

"Oh, come on!" Ben said. He looked around at the others. "I'm not crazy. I don't lie out in the sun in that desert. You know that."

"Mr. O'Neil," Barowitz said, "didn't you tell me that one time when you were in the helicopter you saw this man lying nude in the desert?"

"Well," Denny said, not looking at Ben, "I don't know whether he was absolutely nude."

Ben stared at Denny until he at last looked at him. "Thanks a lot," Ben said.

"I didn't know he was going to twist it around like that," Denny said.

Barowitz looked at Ben. "Do you deny Mr. O'Neil's testimony?"

Ben slumped in his chair. "One time, I was trying to find out how a vulture would react to a body lying on the desert," he said tonelessly.

"Oh, I see," Barowitz said. "You weren't taking a sunbath?"

"I wasn't taking a sunbath."

"Just lying there waiting to be devoured by the vultures?"

Ben saw some of them smile.

Barowitz turned away. "Now, Doctor," he said pleasantly, "you've detailed the minor cuts and bruises of this man, but what of my . . ."

Hondurak interrupted him by saying, "Doctor, didn't you put in your report that Ben had been shot, too?"

"Yes, in the arm."

"And a very interesting wound it is," Barowitz said, "I suggest you take a look at it, sir."

Ben held up his arm, turning it so that the two bandages could be seen.

"Isn't that a convenient little wound?" Barowitz asked. "The kind of minor flesh wound a man would inflict on himself in an attempt to accuse someone of shooting him. As you say in your report, Doctor, the bullet caused no injury to his arm. It's evident, sir, that this man shot himself, being very careful not to hurt himself, and only for the purpose of trying to incriminate Mr. Madec."

"Mr. Hondurak, how did I do that, if I didn't have a gun?" Ben asked.

Barowitz said smoothly, "Sir, it has already been established that he did have a gun, that he took his rifle with him. That's how he was able to see the warden's clothes—with the telescopic sight."

"Oh, that's right," Hondurak said.

Barowitz turned back to the doctor. "Now let's get on to real evidence. The intentional, deliberate, premeditated—and actual—shooting of Mr. Madec by this man, who now claims that he didn't have a gun. I'm sure, Doctor, that you can prove to any court's satisfaction that Mr. Madec was shot, and shot repeatedly, with malice and with forethought."

"I don't know what the man who shot him was thinking about," the doctor said. "I can only testify that Mr. Madec was shot. Five times."

"Five times," Barowitz said slowly, and looked around at the men in the room. "Since all of you are expert marksmen I'm sure you'll all agree with me that an expert who hits a man five times in five shots, but does not kill him, evidently did not *want* to kill him. That, in fact, to have killed him would have been a fatal error."

"I didn't want to kill him," Ben said. "You don't have to prove that."

"Of course you didn't!" Barowitz snapped at him. "Or you wouldn't have any alibi at all."

He turned back to the doctor. "What caliber rifle was Madec shot with, Doctor?"

Ben eased his head back on the chair. "He wasn't shot with any caliber rifle. He was . . ."

"Ben," Hondurak warned. "Go ahead, Doctor."

"I'm not an expert on calibers," the doctor said. "All I have is evidence of what hit Mr. Madec."

Barowitz took a Hornet cartridge out of his pocket and showed it to the doctor. "About the same size, same diameter, as this bullet?"

The doctor examined the bullet and said, "Very close, I'd say."

"That's a Hornet bullet, so wouldn't you say that Mr. Madec was shot by a Hornet rifle, Doctor?"

Before he could answer, Hondurak said mildly, "Isn't that kind of assuming things?"

"If that's your opinion, sir," Barowitz said. "All I'm trying to establish is that the doctor said Mr. Madec was hit by bullets of the same size as a Hornet's. I really don't think you could call that an assumption."

"Well, I don't know. Let it pass for now," Hondurak said.

"Of course, sir. Now, Doctor, aren't the bullets that hit Mr. Madec the same caliber as those that hit and killed the old man? Hornet bullets?"

"Two of the slugs you showed me are about the same size, but smaller than the third."

Ben's uncle looked confused. "Third? I

thought he was only shot twice."

Barowitz sounded a little tired as he said, "Don't you remember? Your nephew also used Mr. Madec's gun to shoot the old man."

"Oh, that's right," Ben's uncle said.

"Three times," the doctor said. "Once by a bullet of considerable weight, traveling at high speed. The other two wounds were made by bullets of much less weight."

That made Barowitz happy. "A good doctor doesn't need an autopsy to make a simple observation like that, does he, Doctor?"

"No. You can look at the wounds and see the difference in tissue and bone destruction made by a heavy bullet, compared to that of a much lighter bullet."

Hondurak would just tell him to shut up again, Ben thought, but he asked it anyway. "Which one killed him, Doc?"

The doctor looked at him as though he were an idiot. "The first one to hit him, of course."

"Then either the bullet in his throat or the one in his chest could have killed him?" Barowitz asked.

"The one in the chest," the doctor said.

Ben pushed his aching feet out along the floor and slumped down in the chair, knowing that the doctor would ignore him. "Which one, Doc? The little one or the big one?"

Ben was surprised when the doctor said quietly, "Of the two bullets that hit him in the chest, the first one killed him. That was the heavier of the two."

Ben jerked his legs back and sat up straight, waiting for their reaction.

But Barowitz said smoothly, "Now coming back to the injuries sustained by my client, Doctor, would you say they are serious enough to be considered an attempt on his life?"

Ben couldn't stand this any longer. "*Wait* a minute!" he said, trying to get on his feet. "Didn't any of you hear what he said? Weren't you *listening*?"

"Ben . . ." the sheriff growled.

"He was killed by the .358!" Ben yelled. "Madec killed him! Can't you see that?"

"You killed him," Strick said, coming over to him and standing in front of him. "You killed him with Mr. Madec's gun so you could blame it on Madec."

"Shut up, Strick," Ben said, and hobbled around him to the doctor. Putting his hand on the doctor's arm, he said, "Doctor, help me."

"What do you think I'm doing?" the doctor snapped.

Ben stared at him. "You're putting me in jail."

"I'll be the judge of that," the doctor said.

Ben let his hand drop. "All right, so just tell them again that the .358 killed him."

"I don't even know what .358 signifies," the doctor said.

"It's a bullet," Ben said. "And it killed him.

Why can't you say that again?"

Barowitz stepped past Ben to Hondurak. "Isn't it really immaterial, your honor, which bullet killed him? Isn't the material thing here not what, but *who?*"

"Yeah," Hondurak said vaguely. Then he leaned around Barowitz and said, "Doc, how do you know which one killed him? I mean, how can you tell?"

"Doctor!" Barowitz said coldly, "I advise you not to answer that. It's a question for a forensic pathologist, not a general practitioner." Then he turned to Hondurak. "I appreciate the doctor's efforts to clear up this matter, but of course you realize that only an experienced pathologist could determine a thing like that."

"Let me talk a little," Hondurak said. "Doc, you said the .358 killed him. Can you back that up, or not?"

"The heaviest bullet killed him," the doctor said.

"You embarrass me, Doctor," Barowitz said. "And you embarrass your profession. You are not competent to make such an assumption."

The doctor went on talking to Hondurak as though Barowitz hadn't said anything. "The first bullet to hit that old man was the heaviest of the three that hit him. I don't know the name of it —.358—Hornet—but it was the bullet that killed him."

Barowitz flung out his arms. "Inadmissible! Conclusion! Assumption!"

The doctor paid no attention to him. "The other two bullets did not hurt that old man at all. . . ."

"Not hurt! . . . In the throat? . . ." Barowitz screamed. "In the chest . . ."

"He was dead," the doctor said calmly. "When those two bullets struck him he had been dead for almost an hour."

Ben could feel that statement hitting everybody in the room. They moved, sitting up straighter, listening, looking.

Barowitz' voice broke the silence as he said quietly, "Doctor, did you have, as required by law, the family's permission to perform an autopsy on that man?"

"No autopsy," the doctor said.

"Doctor," Barowitz said in a pained voice, "I've had years of court experience with some of the world's leading doctors in forensic medicine so I hope you won't continue this line of absurd assumptions and guesses. You are making statements of fact that could only be determined after a complete autopsy by a competent pathologist."

The doctor didn't even look at Barowitz. "When a bullet hits a living man, he bleeds," the doctor said. "But after a man dies the functions of his body stop, his heart stops, blood stops moving in his veins and arteries. His tissues die, and after he's been dead for a little while he can no longer bleed. Two wounds in that old man, made by smaller, lighter weight bullets, caused no bleeding, either internally or externally. Which proves that he had been dead for some time before they hit him."

"Mr. Hondurak," Barowitz said, going toward the table, "I'm sure that a justice of your experience realizes how embarrassing it would be for you to present this sort of incompetent, inadmissible and arrogant testimony to the court. I would strongly suggest, sir, that you strike all of this doctor's testimony from the record and, to save further embarrassment, that we listen to no more of it."

"You mean," Hondurak said vaguely, "that because he's not a pathologist, only a doctor, he doesn't know about that sort of thing?"

"Exactly, sir. I'm very glad you see it my way."

"Well . . ." Hondurak said, looking up at the ceiling. "I don't think I see it all your way. Doc, you got anything else you want to say?"

"Not much," the doctor said.

Barowitz cut in, his voice very affable. "No one could object to the doctor going on with his nonsense. But to save ourselves embarrassment, sir, it shouldn't be a part of the record."

Sonja looked up from her machine, but Hondurak said, "Oh, take it down, Sonja. I don't embarrass easy."

The doctor was rooting around among the instruments in his pocket but at last found what he was looking for and held it out to Hondurak. "I extracted this from the wound in Mr. Madec's right wrist."

"What's that?" the sheriff asked, coming over to look at what the doctor was holding. "That's a buckshot!" he said. "Looks like about a double-O buckshot to me."

"It is," Ben said. "It's what I used in the slingshot."

"Of course," Barowitz said. "That nonexistent slingshot. Your honor, I don't like to say this, but don't you think that there's collusion here between the doctor and the accused? A doctor can produce any sort of object and claim he extracted it from the wound of a victim."

"If there's any collusion," the doctor said, "Emma William's in on it, too. She's the one who first saw this thing. I only took it out."

Hondurak reached over and picked up the buckshot. "What do you make of it, Ham?"

"Well, I don't know," the sheriff said. "Ben says he only hit him with a slingshot, and if the bullet was still in Madec's wrist it couldn't have been going very fast."

"Was it inside his wrist, Doc?" Hondurak asked. "Not just lying around somewhere?"

"It was embedded in the tendons of Mr. Madec's wrist. His other wounds were also made by soft lead projectiles, not by bullets with brass cases like those I've been shown, because there are traces of lead in all his wounds."

Barowitz pushed roughly past the doctor to confront Hondurak. "Your honor, I have to object! You can't let this man continue his contrived assumptions as to weapon and ammunition when all he has produced is a common buckshot, available in any dime store."

As Barowitz talked, the doctor rooted around in the big pocket again.

At first Ben thought it was one of his surgical instruments, the metal shining in the light. And then he saw the rubber tubes, the little leather pouch.

The doctor tapped Barowitz on the back with the butt of the slingshot. "And this . . ."

Barowitz didn't look around as he said, "For your own position, sir, you should strike all this from the record."

The sheriff took the slingshot and said, "Where'd you get this, Doc?"

"Out of the trash basket. In the emergency room. I saw Madec throw something away when he first came in, and when I found the shot, I wondered," the doctor said.

At last Barowitz turned around. He looked at the slingshot for a moment and then looked around at all the people looking at him.

There was a dead silence in the room for a long time and then Hondurak said, "Les, how about you and Denny going out in the morning and see if you can find anything in that tunnel —bird bones, maybe a lizard skin. . . ."

Barowitz' voice sounded mechanical. "I have already established that dead birds prove nothing."

They weren't listening to him any more as Hondurak went on. ". . . and maybe Ben left some blood across that funnel. Wouldn't be any other way to get it there."

Les didn't seem to be listening to anything. He sat, his legs stretched out in front of him, frowning down at the floor. Then at last he looked up. "I could kick myself," Les said, and then turned to Ben. "Ben, I'm sorry. I apologize. I could just kick myself. Judge, when I was at the Jeep talking to Madec, Ben couldn't have had his gun up in the mountains or anywhere else. I just remember now that I saw that old Hornet of Ben's in the windshield scabbard of the Jeep."

Hondurak said to the sheriff, "Ham, we'd better keep that deputy on duty down there with Mr. Madec. Yeah, we'd better do that."

Barowitz was shaking. "Don't think for a minute that this is the end of this!"

"Well, I don't think it is, Mr. Barowitz," Hondurak said mildly.

Barowitz whirled away from him, and the two lawyers walked out of the room, their briefcases swinging in unison.

Nobody said anything. Nobody even looked at Ben. His uncle was looking up at the ceiling and Les was pulling at a loose thread in his pants and Denny was examining the floor and Sonja was putting a cover on her stenotype machine and Strick was cleaning something off the butt of his gun with his fingernail and the sheriff was showing the doctor how to hold the slingshot and Hondurak was pushing some papers into a pile.

And then, at last, Hondurak looked up at Ben. "Ben, you see, it was just so hard for me to believe that any man could do the things he did to another man. I just couldn't believe it, Ben."

"Neither could I," Ben said.

Hondurak looked vaguely around the room. "We'll have to charge Mr. Madec with something. . . . Aggravated assault? . . ." He looked at Ben. "He tried to kill you, didn't he, Ben? He shot you. So, will you testify to intent to commit murder and assault with a deadly weapon?"

"No," Ben said. "I came in here to report an accident."